Vicky
So glad to see you @FBBF 2019.
Hope you love Dustan
♡ Measha Stone

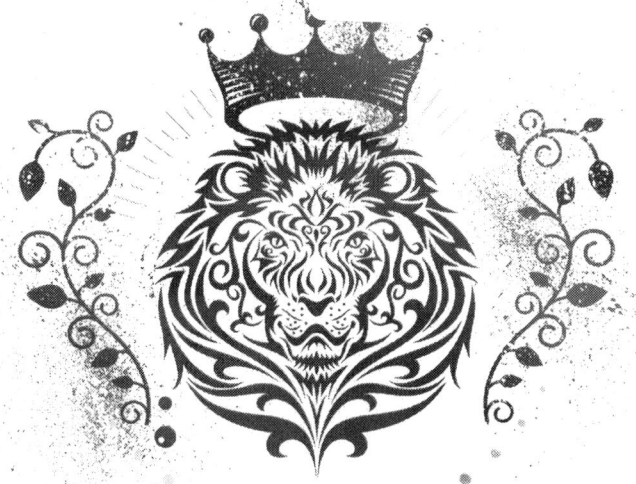

VALOR

Cavalieri Della Morte

MEASHA STONE

Copyright © 2019 by Measha Stone
Published by Measha Stone
Cover Designer - Jay Aheer (Simply Defined Art)
All rights reserved, including the right to reproduce this book or portions thereof in any form whatsoever.
The following story contains mature themes, strong language, and sexual situations. It is intended for adult readers.
No part of this book may be reproduced or transmitted in any form or by any means, electronic or mechanical, including photocopying, recording, or by any information storage and retrieval system, without permission in writing. If you would like to share this book with another person, please purchase an additional copy for each recipient. If you're reading this book and did not purchase it, or it was not purchased for your enjoyment only, then please purchase your own copy. Thank you for respecting the hard work of this author.

This book is a work of fiction. Names, characters, places, and incidents either are products of the author's imagination or are used fictitiously. Any resemblance to actual events or locales or persons, living or dead, is entirely coincidental.

The author acknowledges the trademarked status and trademark owners of various products referenced in the work of fiction, which have been used without permission. The publication/use of these trademarks is not authorized, associated with, or sponsored by the trademark owner.

DUSTAN

Smokers huddled around each other the required fifty feet away from the doors to the bar, puffing away on their cigarettes and electronic nicotine dispensers. I hated the smell of smoke, it reminded me of dirtier times of my life. Times best left smashed at the bottom of an ashtray.

I walked past them, turning my head to breathe fresh air, and headed up the two steps into the bar. A local joint. Music blasted from the digital jukebox in the back corner, pool tables crowded with what were probably the usuals, but I wasn't interested in any of that. What I had my eye on hadn't arrived yet.

But he would.

Like clockwork, Antonio Merde would walk through the front door and find his stool at the bar. He'd order his usual bourbon on the rocks and sip it while he eyed the sweet candy walking around the bar.

I knew this because it's my job to know. Every move Antonio had made in the last week had been categorically noted in my head. It made it easier that the man was an idiot and never varied his routine. He did the same shit every single day. No changes, no variations. It made my job a little too easy.

Which put me on edge because it shouldn't be so fucking easy. Antonio had connections. Strong ties to bad men. He should have known better. But he was also a second cousin, making him far from the head of the family. Maybe he didn't have the brains his uncle hoped he'd have when he put him in charge of distribution on the East Coast.

Not completely in charge. I found that out, too.

Antonio shared his power with his younger brother. A kick in the nuts, probably, but that wasn't why I was sitting in the bar, waiting. I had something else altogether to discuss with him.

A few of the smokers filed in, admitting the chilled air from outside. Winter hadn't settled in completely, but fall had been a real bitch. If it wasn't raining, it was balls cold, but since I was on site doing my job, the weather wasn't really taking up much of my focus.

The guys cleared past me, reeking of smoke or whatever flavor vape shit they'd just ruined their lungs with, and I caught sight of someone worth a moment of my time. At least a quick look.

Most of the women in there were partnered up with someone, or at least openly on the prowl. They'd put on their warpaint and doused themselves in their favorite scents. Perfect curls or tight buns were placed, and outfits I'm sure they took more than an hour choosing donned. But not her—she was different.

She walked behind the smokers, but she wasn't with any of them. Her hair was pulled back into a loose ponytail at her nape. Strands had fallen out, framing her delicate features. She had curves. I could see them despite the loose-fitting blouse and flowing skirt. Fuck, if I had a thing for schoolgirls, this girl would be right on the money. Give her a pair of thick—rimmed glasses, and she'd be textbook school—girl.

I gripped my glass of whiskey and took a sip just as her eyes caught mine. I hardened my stare. As fuckable as she seemed, I didn't have time tonight. I had a job to do.

But unlike most girls who took the sign to turn away and keep moving, this girl smiled. I swallowed my sip, letting the burn of the whiskey become front and center in my mind. Because she headed in my direction.

She wiggled her way between me and the stool beside me, her elbow perched on the bar and her face turned up. I had at least a full head on her. If I stood up, would she even reach my shoulders?

"You look like you don't want to be bothered," she said softly, her gaze roaming my face and down my torso.

"And yet, here you are." I tried to present a firm expression, but she was already giggling at my words. The sound didn't fit her. Like she'd forced it from a mental script.

"I don't really want to be bothered, either." She turned full frontal to the bar and waved down the bartender, rising on tiptoe until her breasts rested on the bar. "Can I get a whiskey sour, please?" she asked in the sweetest voice I'd heard in too long. But it was fake. What game was she playing at?

"Sure thing, sweetheart." The bartender didn't

even try to hide his assessment of her breasts on his bar. With a quick swipe of his tongue over his lips, he darted off to make her drink.

"If you don't want to be bothered, you probably shouldn't be so—up front," I pointed out, sipping again. If I finished my drink too fast, I'd want another one. And it was a one—drink sort of night.

"His attention is fine. He'll be heavy-handed with my drink, and he'll use the good stuff. But all these other assholes?" She waved a hand at the rest of the bar. "I'd rather they just stay where they are."

"So, you're using me as a shield." I couldn't help but smile. It was a first for me.

"Yeah. You have that scary sort of look. These guys aren't going to mess with me if they think I'm talking to you." She lifted a shoulder in a shrug. Her fingers trembled on the bar top, and her eyes didn't quite meet mine.

"Here you go." The bartender put a small napkin on the bar then placed her drink. "Eight fifty," he announced, leaning closer to her than I liked. He was trying to get a glimpse down her blouse. Prick.

She twisted her little black purse from around her neck and pulled out a ten. "Here you go. No change." She waved the bill at him then handed it off. The bartender winked and headed back down to other patrons not as patient for his attention.

She took a sip of her drink and smiled up at me. "See? Not watered down, and top shelf."

I started to say something, but my guy walked in. I checked my watch. He was a few minutes early. He made his way to his usual stool, and the guy already sitting there got up and wordlessly moved to another seat.

I knew his routine. He'd order and then hit the head. I had at least fifteen minutes before I needed to get up. So, I sipped my drink and watched the woman enjoy hers.

"I know why I don't want to be dealing with all these jerks, but what about you? Just hiding out after a long day at the office?" Her fingers flicked over the lapel of my suit jacket. I was overdressed for the atmosphere. I knew it but didn't give a fuck. Traditions needed to be kept. And when on a job, I dress for work.

"Yeah, something like that," I acknowledged and swung my gaze back to Antonio. He had his glass in hand. Not too much longer.

"So, what do you do? This part of the city, I wouldn't expect to see a financial guy." She forced another giggle and sipped again, her gaze roaming over me again. Assessing. This woman searched me for something.

"Market's not my thing." I shook my head,

checking my watch. Just another minute and I'd have to get up from my stool.

She sipped again, and I watched her thick lips as the liquor slipped past them. I wondered for a quick beat if her lips were warm, or would they be frigid if I kissed her?

"What about you?" I turned the topic on her. I couldn't exactly go into details of my work, and I was actually curious what this beauty did during the day.

"Oh, office work." She shrugged again, brushing off the topic, too. Fine. I'm good with a little mystery. It's not like anything was happening there, or later.

Antonio got up, laughing at something the guy next to him said. He slapped the guy on his back and waved to the bartender, calling for another round. After his second glass, I knew he'd slip out the back and head home. Antonio never left through the front. Probably convinced someone watched his moves, but he was probably thinking more the FBI than me. I'm not FBI. I'm not anything that can be traced.

I kept my eyes on the girl but my focus on Antonio's movements. After he made a stop at the bathroom, he'd meet his contact in the back room for five minutes, make his collection for the week, and get his ass back to his stool. The collections happened every Friday night. I didn't give a shit about that, though. I just needed the timeline to stay the same. If he stayed on schedule, everything would go off without a hitch.

"You need another?" she asked, pointing at my drink. I only had a sip left.

"I'm good," I said, rolling my shoulders. "You?" I asked when she downed the rest of hers.

"Yeah. I think so. It's been a rough day." She nodded, but the tremor from her hands showed up in her voice. She wasn't drinking off a stressful day; she was gulping down courage.

"Oh yeah?" I said with a raised hand. I couldn't imagine her having a rough day, not with the sweet composure she'd walked in with. If she was going to lie, she needed to get better at it.

"Another?" the bartender asked, his expression a little less enthusiastic now that I was the one calling him over and not her breasts.

"Sure. Thanks." She smiled at him but without all the promise she had before. Maybe she was looking for the watered-down drink now.

I pulled out my wallet just as Antonio brushed past us and headed back to his stool. I tossed a ten on the counter, and the bartender swiped it up in his palm.

"You don't have to do that," she said but didn't reach into her purse. I lifted the corner of my mouth and nodded.

"Not a problem."

"I'm Cherry," she said with a bright smile, but it didn't quite light up her eyes. Her hand thrust out at me, and I found myself wrapping my fingers around it.

"Cherry?" I asked holding back my laugh. Of course, it wasn't, but she stuck to her game plan. Give her some pigtails and a lollipop and we could have ourselves a real old-fashioned porno.

"Yeah. Silly, I know." Her thumb rubbed against mine, and I realized I was still touching her. She was warm and smooth. Her grip wasn't as firm as mine but not weak. She was no pushover. "And yours?"

Mine. She wanted my name.

I glanced over at Antonio as he downed his drink and checked his watch, not in the social mood tonight. He was making to leave.

"Dustan," I said, slipping my wallet back in my

pocket and touching my hand to the handle of my Glock. Antonio was up and saying his goodbyes. It was a fast night for him.

He slapped the back of a few more guys, pointed and laughed at one of the men, and fidgeted with his coat. He ran his hand through his hair, like he was getting ready for a date, but that wasn't happening. Not tonight.

Or any other night.

Cherry started talking again, and I nodded along, keeping eye contact but focused on Antonio. He would be out the back door in a few moments. I had to get gone.

"I'm gonna take a piss," I said, standing. Cherry stepped back, her jaw slack, but she didn't grab for me, though for a split second, I thought she was going to. I headed down the corridor toward the bathrooms and walked right past them, past the offices, and through the back door into the crisp night air.

I walked a ways down the alley, toward the end that intersected with another. Antonio had an odd way about him, and he really shouldn't be walking through dark alleys alone when he had so much betrayal weighing on his head.

Finding the spot I'd picked out, I pressed myself against the building. Antonio would walk to the end of the alley and make a right turn. His car was parked on the other side of the last building. He took the same walk every time he made his collection. Maybe he liked the threat of being jumped. A little adrenaline rush after pocketing his skim of the take.

The back door of the bar opened, and he stepped out. The overhanging lighting was out, but I could make him out fine. His cough signaled his proximity, and I was ready for him. It would be clean and over within a second; he just needed to take a few more steps.

His phone fucking rang, and he stopped to answer. I managed to keep my annoyance to myself. I couldn't take care of him while he was on the fucking phone. I needed him to hang up. He got closer, still chatting away on the line. A date. He was making plans for a fuck fest on my time.

My jaw ached, and I forced my muscles to unclench. Being tense wouldn't help the situation. This wasn't a hard task. Probably the easiest I'd had in a long time. Arthur could have given this job to anyone with less experience, but I had the time. Plus, I fucking hated thieves. Stealing for survival was one thing, skimming off the top from your own family was stomach turning.

Antonio hung up but was in the middle of tapping on his screen when I stepped out of my cloaked space. He paused, looked up with surprise.

The alley was almost always empty. It wasn't exactly a shady part of town, and a lot of his associates hung out in the surrounding businesses. Common criminals didn't linger trying to take down these guys.

But I wasn't a common criminal.

"Who the fuck—" His question wasn't finished before the bullet cracked through his skull. He crumpled, knees hit the concrete first then facedown into a puddle.

A sound from behind me pulled my attention. A sharp click of heels moved along the ground. My eyes adjusted to the lack of lighting in the alley, and I saw her.

Cherry.

She took small steps backward, back to the bar door.

Fuck.

Loose ends don't work for me. And she was a very

loose end.

I left Antonio. Someone else could deal with him. Man like him ended up dead in an alley, there would be questions but quietly ignored. My problem was in front of me, making her way back to the bar.

Her wide eyes were aimed at me, but she wasn't meeting my gaze. Probably had something to do with the way I stalked after her, my gun still in my hand, ready to finish what she'd started.

A shame, really.

She was gorgeous.

But that changed nothing.

"Cherry." I raised my gun, pointing it at her. "Come back here, Cherry," I ordered, keeping my voice soft but commanding.

She reached behind her, fumbling for the doorknob.

"I just came out for some fresh air," she lied.

"Come here," I said again, lowering my gun a fraction.

She used the moment to yank the door open. I lunged forward as her purse snagged on the knob. She moved too fast, and the strap broke. I didn't follow her inside. She'd be too frightened to stop and tell anyone what she'd seen—at least right then. So, I didn't pursue. Too many of Antonio's friends were in there anyway. I had kept a low profile, so far. Chasing a girl through the bar—that would have sparked some memories later on if questions were asked.

I picked up her abandoned purse. It was heavy in my palm. After I inspected the contents, my heart slowed back down. Her wallet was not inside, but her phone was.

Cherry could run for now.

I'd find her easily enough.

CHERISE

Heated rays of sun burst through the blinds and ripped me from sleep. Not that it was the greatest night's sleep I'd had, but at least I'd finally stopped panicking and had fallen asleep.

Rubbing my face, I sat up. All the worry from last night poured back into my brain, setting off another race between my heart and my lungs. Whichever one won would get to keep working.

I'd been so stupid. So flipping idiotic, thinking I could do it. I should have known the moment I laid eyes on that man. Danger illuminated the space around him. Nothing about him had given me the impression talking to him, much less following him outside, was safe.

I clenched my eyes closed again, reliving the moment. The shot, the blood spray. If I'd been a few feet closer, I probably would have been covered with it. The sound, that awful thump of a body crumpling to the ground.

And his voice.

That controlled, deep tenor that made my insides melt and my skin electrify. His gun had been pointed at me. Me. I had been seconds away from being killed.

Enough!

I threw the covers back and climbed out of bed. Sitting around thinking about what could have happened was only going to keep me scared. The idea behind going out the night before had been to get out of my safe zone, to stop being so scared of meeting people.

I eyed the book on my nightstand. *Climbing Out*

of Your Shell. Stupid book. I should have stayed in my shell. Safely tucked away in my apartment where men like Dustan didn't live.

I needed to pee and shower. Then I needed to get my ass to the store and buy a new phone. Thankfully, I'd been smart enough to tuck my wallet away in the inside pocket of my skirt. Other than a few bills and my phone, I hadn't lost anything when I left my purse behind. At least he didn't have my address.

Music filled the bathroom while I showered. I lost myself beneath the warm stream of the water, or at least tried to. I still felt shaky when I thought about running through that bar and hailing a cab. I had kept looking over my shoulder, expecting him to step out of the bar with that gun aimed at me again. The poor cab driver must have thought I was a real nutcase, the way I'd thrown myself into the back of his car and shouted at him to drive.

I needed a distraction. I couldn't keep reliving the event. I'd go mad. It was done with. I saw what I saw, and I was not going to tell anyone. I knew enough to keep silent. There would be no calls to the police or statements given. As far as I knew, nothing had happened in that alley. There was no man named Dustan, and he definitely didn't shoot anyone.

I turned off the radio and made my way back to my bedroom with a towel snugly wrapped around my body. Even alone in my apartment, I couldn't stride around naked. I really needed more help than any self-help book could provide.

The blinds were closed when I stepped back into my bedroom. I paused in the doorway, not remembering having closed them. Taking a deep breath, I reminded myself the doors were locked, and I was fine. No one was in the apartment.

Growing up in a small town in Minnesota hadn't

prepared me for life in Chicago, but I needed to get over my skittish nature. This was my chance to make something of myself. My one shot at getting out of a farm town and being something more.

I grabbed a pair of jeans and a sweater from my dresser drawers and tossed them on the bed. A cold shiver ran down my spine when I opened my panty drawer. I wasn't alone, and no matter how much I tried to convince myself otherwise, I knew it.

Slowly, I looked up at myself in the mirror hanging over my dresser.

Dustan.

I gasped, strangled myself with air was really how it felt, but the result was the same. His lips, the ones I had found so appealing the night before, curled up at the edges. It wasn't a pleased smile or even a grin. My fear fed him.

"Morning, darlin'." He stood behind me, looking

at my mirrored image. How had he moved so silently?

My lip trembled while my mind screamed to every part of my body to move, to run, get away from him. Yet, there I stood. Frozen with a pair of purple cotton briefs in my hand.

"Not happy to see me?" He tilted his head to the right.

"I—I uh, how did you find me?"

He lifted my cell phone so I could see it then reached around my body, making sure to brush his muscular arm against mine, and dropped it on the dresser. I stared at it as though it were going to stand up and bite my nose off.

"Technology is amazing," he said. "Would have had more trouble finding you with your driver's license than your phone." He was lying. He had to be. That couldn't be true.

"Why, why are you here?" I asked, still fisting my

underwear and watching his face in the mirror. Defined features. His chin and nose had sharp angles, but that wasn't what made him look so damn fierce. His eyes did that. The way the deep brown of them warmed as he stared at me. Not the chocolate—chip melty sort of warm, but the confident, arrogant sort of heat.

"Well, we didn't get to finish our conversation last night." He stepped back from me. I turned around to face him, not liking him at my back. He walked over to the bed and hopped on, crossing his ankles and leaning against my headboard.

"I got the sense you were busy." I tried to smile, to take the moment as casually as he was doing, but I couldn't get my lips to turn up. They were too busy trying not to open wide and vomit all over his shoes. And although he would deserve it for breaking into my apartment and scaring me, he probably wouldn't take it with any sort of grace.

"Hmm, yeah, that's what we need to talk about." He rested his hands in his lap, and that's when I noticed he had his gun with him. In his lap. My stomach rolled up and down and then took a nosedive just to add something special to the panic building inside me.

"I don't think we do. I don't think there's anything to talk about at all. I think we can just go our separate ways, like we never met. Because, really, we didn't. Not truly," I rambled. Some people fainted when they reached the level of fear bubbling through my veins, but I apparently threw up words.

"Oh, but we did meet, Cherise," he said using my full name. My real name. Cherry had been another stupid idea from the book. *Pick something fun, something that says you're a laid-back person.* I wanted a refund on that book.

My mouth dried when he moved his gun to his left hand and reached over to the side table, picking up the book. Fear wasn't enough, humiliation needed to attend the party as well. I must have looked at it, given myself away. Further proof, I was not cut out for this situation.

"Climbing out of your shell?" He huffed a little laugh and opened the book, flipping through the pages. "Is this what brought you to the bar last night?" he asked, holding the book open with his hand spread out over the spine and turned it at me. He'd flipped right to the chapter I'd read last. The one that gave me the foolish idea that I could actually take a step in becoming more outgoing.

"I—" Flames could have burst from my cheeks at that moment. "Yes. Look. I really don't want any trouble. I don't—I didn't see or hear anything. I just stepped outside for a breath of air, and I went right back in."

"You left your purse behind." He slammed the

book shut. The loud clap made me jump. I grabbed the towel tighter.

"It's just a purse." I shrugged. "No big deal."

He scooted farther down the bed until he sat at the very end. "Come here, darlin'," he said with a crook of his finger.

I couldn't. If I did, he'd grab me. I needed to get away from him.

"Why?" I asked, taking a small step closer to the door.

"'Cause, I said. And it's really better for you to do what I say." His eyes narrowed, and tension built up in his jaw. He hadn't shaved yet. The dark stubble made his already stony face even colder.

"I doubt that." I laughed then dragged in a breath. Laughing at him wouldn't help. He didn't seem the sort to appreciate a joke at a time like this.

"You're gonna have to trust me on this. Come

here." He beckoned me again.

His other hand still held the gun on his leg. Why couldn't he just do it already? He hadn't made the man wait last night. He'd just stepped out and done it. Why was he putting me through the terror first?

I took the three steps toward him; my knees brushed his. His lips spread upward, showing off perfectly straight, white teeth.

"That's a good girl. Let's keep that up, okay?" He slid his finger into the top of my towel. I started to jerk back, but he froze, shooting a glare up at me and making me stop. I pulled in a deep breath through my nose and raised my chin. My insides may be having a conga party, but he didn't get to see it.

His finger snaked between the towel and my skin, between my breasts. I clamped my jaws tight. He slithered to my left breast, where my towel was tucked securely. The end of the cloth pulled free with a small tug, and my hand smacked over his, holding the fabric in place.

"That's not being a good girl, is it?" he asked, his tone getting darker, softer. "Move your hand, Cherise." The order came hard, but he hadn't raised his voice. I got the feeling he never yelled, he didn't need to, not with those impenetrable eyes of his.

"What are you going to do to me?" I asked, hating the little tremor I heard.

"Depends on you." His answer didn't really give any information. Did that mean if I was good, did what he said, he wouldn't hurt me? Or did it mean if I didn't struggle, he'd hurt me less?

"Hands down, Cherise." His chin rose a fraction, and I dropped my hand.

"Good girl," he said again. The two words rolled off his tongue smooth and sweet. The sound of his approval settled the raw edges of my nerves.

He opened the towel and pulled it from my body, dropping it to the floor at my feet, my every tendon cramped up with his eyes on me. He wasn't looking at my face anymore. Not when my breasts bobbed right in front of his eyes.

I must have made a little sound because he shot another glance up at me. "Does this scare you?" he asked, lightly tracing my hip with his fingers. "Being naked?"

"I already told you I won't say anything." I kept my gaze away from him. I stared at the wall, focused on a small spot just over his shoulder.

"I asked you a question, Cherise. Does being nude in front of me scare you?" His fingers stilled on my hip. Heat lingered where he'd touched and burned into my skin where he continued to remain connected to me.

"No," I lied, glad that I managed to keep some of

the fear from my voice.

"Liar." He chuckled. I guess not enough of the tremor had been removed. His touch moved up my body to my breasts, and he ran his fingers beneath them, lightly touching but sending waves of electricity through my body.

My phone buzzed on the dresser, dancing along the top. I turned to grab it, but his fingers dug into my side, pinning me where I stood.

"Leave it," he ground out, lifting his gun from his lap.

"It's probably work. I'm on call this morning," I said quickly. Working as a medical receptionist at the emergency care clinic down the block wasn't exactly my life ambition, but it paid my rent and put food in the fridge.

The phone started dancing again as another text came through. Then another.

"If I don't respond, they'll worry," I lied again. If I didn't answer in five minutes, they went to the next on the call list. I'd lose the extra shift, but no one would come looking for me.

"Pick it up," he said. "Show it to me."

I twisted, grimacing at the pain his grip caused my side, and grabbed the phone. I swiped it open and read the message.

My stomach dropped again, and he was no longer the scariest thing in my life at that moment.

"What is it?" he asked, taking the phone from me. He read through the messages, Claire, the closest thing I had to a friend, sent.

What the fuck happened?

Cherise! Why are the police looking for you!?

Cherise!

Answer me!

Several more messages rang through. The cops

were at the clinic asking after me. Had my picture and wanted my name and address.

"Shit." Dustan dropped my phone and grabbed my arm.

He pulled me into the living room and flicked on my television set, finding the news channel.

There I was.

Security footage of me running down the back hallway and through the bar. It had to be after I'd come back inside from the alley. After I'd seen Dustan.

"Police are looking for this woman," the anchorwoman said, pausing to show a freeze frame of my face. Not the best likeness, but I had been running for my life at the time. "They believe she has information in regard to an investigation for a missing person's report." She went on to discuss Antonio Merde's mysterious disappearance.

"They didn't find his body?" I asked.

"That's your big question?" He flicked the television off. "We have to go."

"What? No." I shook my head and started to yank free of him. "I told you, I won't say a word."

"Get some clothes on." He pushed me back to my bedroom. Every time I paused, he shoved me again.

"I'm not going with you," I vowed. He might have been more convinced if I hadn't been shoving my legs into my jeans.

"Hurry up," he said and plucked his phone from his back pocket. I realized then he hadn't changed from the night before. He still wore his dress slacks and his shirt and tie—he'd left his jacket off though.

"I'm—"

He stepped up to me, grabbing my hair into a thick fist and yanking it back. He leveled his glare on me. His breath was hot and heavy across my face as he let the thick silence between us seep into my mind.

"You are going to be a good girl and do everything I say. If you don't, you're going to have some problems. And you have enough of those right now as it is." He scooped up the sweater from my bed. Shoving it at me, he let go of my hair.

I stumbled back a few steps. When he looked ready to pounce again, I jabbed my hands through the sleeves and yanked the sweater over my head. He went to my closet and threw a pair of running shoes at me.

"Hurry up," he snapped again, with less patience, and stalked out of the bedroom to the front of the apartment again. I eyed the window; I could make a run down the fire escape. Maybe I would get down before he got to me.

"Cherise, put the fucking shoes on," he demanded when he came back into the room and found me daydreaming about escape.

I threw on socks and shoes, messing up the ties

twice before finally getting them secured. Even little tasks were harder with his hot glare on me.

Several thuds on the front door made me freeze. I looked at the hallway. If the cops had just been at my work looking for me, they'd definitely be here by now. I chanced a glance at Dustan. His jaw tightened; his face unreadable. He was either bored or pissed beyond what I could recognize, but either way, he wasn't happy. And the man with the gun should always be happy.

"Fire escape." He blew past me and tugged on the window. "Let's go," he said, waving me forward.

I looked back at the door. The police weren't a bad option for me.

"You go," I said, folding my hands over stomach. More banging on the front door.

"Cherise, come here now." He lifted the gun. I closed my eyes and shook my head. He'd be taking a huge risk shooting me with the police in my hallway.

A heavy sigh. "Fine. Hard way it is, darlin'." I opened eyes just as his fist came flying at me. Stars burst in my vision, and then there was just black.

DUSTAN

"What's up?" Bobby picked up my call with his typical nonchalant attitude. Being hidden well behind the scenes gave him a higher level of comfort.

"Not much." I gripped my cell harder to my ear. "Just Antonio Merde's all over the news broadcast this fucking morning." I didn't keep the bite out of my tone. Bobby should have warned me. That's not information I should have found out on the damn TV.

"Yeah. Saw that." He breathed out. Sometimes, his cavalier attitude seeped beneath my skin.

My package kicked the trunk lid. Bobby needed to talk faster.

I turned my car down another street, getting us as

far away from downtown as possible. If the cops were looking for her, they might soon be looking for me.

"You want to expand on that?" I looked in my rearview to be sure no one followed. We were on the edge of the city, but that didn't mean we weren't seen. Climbing down a fire escape with an unconscious woman draped over my shoulder, might not have gone completely unnoticed.

Cherise pounded on the trunk some more with her feet. I should have taken those damn shoes off her once I had her in the trunk. She was yelling, too, but thanks to the gag I'd been smart enough to use, I couldn't understand her.

"I don't know, man. You are completely wiped from those tapes. There's no sign of you leaving or coming back in or even in the fucking bar itself. They aren't looking for you—they want some girl."

"Yeah, what about her? Why do they want her?"

I asked.

"Not sure yet." I heard his quick fingers flying over a keyboard on his end of the phone. "You find her yet?"

"I have her." I ground my teeth when another round of banging started.

"Okay, then. Problem solved." The key clicking stopped.

"No, Bobby, problem not solved. I need to know why the fuck they want her. What does she have to do with Antonio Merde?" I knew what Bobby was thinking: kill the girl, tie up the loose ends, and there wouldn't be an issue. And he was right. Killing Cherise would solve the problem at hand.

But it was the unforeseen issues I worried about. Someone wanted her brought in; someone thought she had something to do with Antonio, and I needed to know who that someone was.

"Dustan, you had your orders; you carried them out. Leave the rest be," Bobby said.

In truth, he was right. Arthur had sent my assignment, and I'd carried it out. Antonio wouldn't be found, not in my lifetime, anyway. Nothing would trace back to Arthur or his organization. I was in the clear. Walking away now made sense.

"Get me more information, Bobby. I want to know who is behind tracking her down and why."

An annoyed sigh rang through the phone. He didn't approve, but I didn't pay him to approve of my decisions. I paid for results.

"Will do. Gonna take some time. Give me a few hours." The key strokes started up again. "What are you going to do with her?"

Now, there was a good question.

"I have a place. Just get the information for me." I hung up before he could make any more attempts to get my head on straight.

After tossing my cell into the console, I turned the radio on, flipping the volume higher than comfortable. She could kick and give muffled screams all she wanted, but I didn't need to listen to it.

By the time I pulled up the ramp into the garage, she'd stopped kicking the trunk. Probably wore herself out. Though I had to give her credit, she'd put up more of a fight than I thought she could.

When she found me in her bedroom, I thought she was going to faint. The color bled from her face so fast, I was ready to catch her in a free fall. The girl from the bar wasn't in that apartment. But finding that self-help book explained that easily. The little dove was figuring out her wings.

And now they'd probably have to be clipped.

I turned off the ignition and sat in the car enjoying the moment of silence. After dealing with Antonio's body, I'd had to start looking for Cherise. I hadn't had a moment of rest since pulling that fucking trigger.

The kicking started again, and my jaw clenched.

"Enough!" I yelled at the back of my sedan.

After popping open my door, I climbed out. Making my way to the trunk, I undid the buttons at my wrists and folded my sleeves up to my elbows.

A surprised yelp answered me when I banged my fist on the top of the trunk. "I'm opening up. Keep your fucking feet down. Got me?" I yelled.

A muffled sound came back at me.

I pulled the trunk open and looked down at my little captive. Her hair was all over the place, either from all the wiggling she did trying to find a good spot to lie or because of the straps from the ball gag. Spit ran down her chin, over her cheek, and pooled beneath her head from the gag. But it was her eyes that caught my complete attention. Blue. Not ocean or sky blue, but with a little mix of green, almost teal. But it wasn't even the odd coloring that kept me focused, it was the wide-eyed, furious fear staring up at me.

Obviously, she was scared, but she was doing her damnedest to hide it from me. Where was the sobbing mess, I'd been sure I'd find? She'd been so timid when she found me in her bedroom. But this girl, this trapped and bound girl, she was ready to battle me.

I looked forward to it.

"Let's get you out." I reached in and grabbed hold of her arms, yanked her up to a sitting position then dragged her over my shoulder until I had her clear of the trunk and back onto her feet.

I felt her movements and fisted her hair before she had a chance to get a step away.

"I wouldn't start doing stupid shit, Cherise," I said, jerking her back against my chest. I let my breath wash over the shell of her ear, let her feel my heat and my presence. Made her understand, she wasn't getting away.

She mumbled from behind the gag. Fast talking, but none of it made sense. I spun her around to face me.

"Get on your knees," I said and shoved her to the ground. I'd left her feet unbound, but her hands were taped in front of her.

She grimaced when her knees hit the concrete garage floor. Another round of muttering came flying at me. From the fear overtaking her eyes, she was begging. She'd promise anything at a time like that, but it wasn't her promises I wanted. Although my cock wasn't displeased with the sight before me.

Tears built up before finally slipping down her cheeks while she continued to ramble behind the tape. The longer I watched her, felt her anxiety ramp up, the faster and louder the sounds came.

"Shhhhhh…" I held one finger over my lips, cupping her chin with my other hand, pushing her head back so I could see straight into her eyes. Another set of tears rolled down her face, chasing each other through the wet tracks.

Her gaze flicked away from my face for a brief moment, just long enough to find my gun strapped at my side. Her struggles increased, so I gripped her chin harder.

"Shhhh, darlin'. No more of that." My voice stayed low, counteracting her borderline hysteria. Those sweet eyes of hers flew from my gun to my face and back again. "I need you to listen now. Can you do that? Can you be a good girl and stop all this noise?" I traced my finger along her jawline.

A soft whimper escaped from behind the gag, and she nodded.

"Okay, good." I dropped my hand from her chin.

"Now. It seems you've stepped into a bit of a mess. I don't know how big the mess is yet, or how you're involved. But, until I know everything, you're staying with me."

She started to shake her head with muffled arguments spewing from behind the gag. I grabbed her hair, fisting it hard, and yanked her back. "I said to keep the noise down." She reacted to my hard tone: her lids widened, and the sounds stopped. A tremor worked its way through her, beneath my grip.

"I need to ask you a few questions. To do that, I have to take your gag out. If you do anything outside what I tell you, there will be serious consequences." I tilted my head, imagining those tears dripping off her chin attesting to something entirely different. Her palpable fear fed me, filled the evil pit inside me, and I wanted more. But, first, I had work.

I released her hair and let her give me the nod

I knew she would. She didn't understand everything going on around her, not yet. The amount of danger coming at her, hell, just in my garage, didn't register with her. Not accurately.

"I'm taking it off." I reached behind her and worked the buckle open, slipping the thin leather straps through it, and pulled the rubber ball from behind her teeth.

"You asshole!" she snapped as soon as the ball was clear. She worked her jaw open and closed and raised her shoulder to wipe her chin.

"Temper temper." I tapped the tip of her nose. "Don't start misbehaving, darlin'." I gave a slow wink, which seemed to piss her off a bit more. Fuck, she was getting fun to play with.

I squatted in front of her, bringing our gazes together. She licked at her lips.

"Who is Antonio Merde?" I asked, leveling my

tone.

She shook her head. "I don't know."

"Now, Cherise, you have to be honest with me, or we're going to have more problems."

"I don't know!" she said with more force. "H-he's the guy you—the guy—the one you went into the alley with." She stammered, but her stare was fierce, locked hard on me. This girl had a fire inside of her, one she had no clue what to do with.

"And what did I do in the alley? What happened to Antonio?" I asked, letting my thumb wander over her jaw. Such smooth skin, unblemished and sweet—much like the girl kneeling before me.

Her eyelids fluttered closed, the dark lashes soaking up the tears dancing on the edges. She took in a shaky breath. I could feel the trembles, the little shocks of adrenaline running through her.

"It's okay." I ran my knuckles across her cheek,

wiping away the tear tracks. "Tell me, Cherise. Tell me the truth. What did I do in the alley with Antonio Merde?"

A sob broke through, and she tried to swallow it back down. It was one thing for her to feel terror, but she seemed determined not to let me see it. If she only knew how transparent she was, I wondered if she would be embarrassed or pissed.

"You shot him." Her voice shook, but her gaze found mine, and her features steadied. Oh, the fear was still there, just below the thin veil of fire. It was taking a lot of her concentration not to crumple at my feet. Most women in her situation would have caved in to their fear a long time ago.

"That's right." I smiled. "Do you think he lived?" I whispered, like I was about to let her in on a secret.

"No." She shook her head slightly. Her eyes still focused on mine, her concentration on trying to keep herself hidden.

"That's right. I killed him." I pulled my Glock from the holster. I loved that gun. Simple and true. Some guys went for the fancy shit. They needed heavy fire power. I didn't need any of that. I just needed the trigger to squeeze tight and the aim to be true. Every time.

Another whimper slid from her lips when I raised the tip of the gun into her eyesight. My finger rested outside the trigger guard, as I had no intention of using it, and you don't touch the trigger unless you're gonna give it a squeeze. But she didn't know that. All she knew was the black, rounded tip of the barrel was in her view.

"And you have that information in that beautiful little head of yours." I touched the barrel to her forehead, dragging it toward her temple to get stray hairs out of the way. Another whimper, louder and coming from lower in her belly.

"I swear—I swear to you." She closed her eyes and pulled in a long breath through her nose, nostrils pinching inward. "I swear I won't tell anyone. I could have—I could have gone to the police last night, and—and I didn't."

"Fair point." I kept the tip of my gun touching her skin, letting her feel the cold metal. "But. There's more here than just you seeing what you shouldn't have. Someone wants to talk to you, and I need to know who that someone is."

"How would I know?" she asked, voice rattling with irritation.

I stared down at her, studying the soft curve of her chin, her short, rounded nose. Even with smeared mascara from the night before, running, mixing with her tears, she was more than a little beautiful. I had noticed it at the bar, but now, seeing the rawness of her features, what I had seen amplified.

I scoffed and dropped my hand to rest on my knee while dragging the barrel of my gun down her face, over her throat, and down to the neckline of her sweater.

A light-purple cotton sweater. Simple and plain. And it matched her panties. I kept my smile to myself over her choice of underwear. We could talk about that later. And we would talk extensively about her panties.

She stilled, probably afraid any movement would make the gun go off. "Understand, darlin', from this moment on, everything you get is at my discretion. Everything from your next meal to your next breath, is all up to me."

I stared back into her eyes, watching her thoughts pass through that pretty head of hers.

"You get that?"

She nodded. "Yes. I understand."

After a moment of silence, I reholstered my gun and moved up to my feet.

"Okay, then. Up." I pulled her onto her feet and dragged her across the garage.

"Where are we going?" she asked when I yanked the back door open.

"Not we, darlin'. You." I found the switch and flipped on the lights, illuminating the cramped cell. The tension in her body told me exactly when her mind registered what she was seeing, and I tightened my grip.

It would be natural for her to try to run away from me. Anyone seeing the concrete floor, metallic tiles on the walls, and the drain in the center of the room would understand it for what it was.

"I—I can't go in there." She tried to pull back from me, but her feet weren't catching well enough on the smooth garage floor to give any real traction.

"Sure, you can." I stepped inside and jerked on her arm, propelling her toward me and then forward. I released her as the momentum took her several steps across the room.

"No no no. *No. No!*" She prepared to lunge for the exit.

"When I have more questions, I'll be back." I smiled. Panic ruled her now, and panic rarely engaged any common sense. I stepped outside and slammed the door.

Fists pounded, but with the soundproofing, all I could make out was a soft thud. Barely audible. If I hadn't been expecting it, would I have even heard it?

I tested the lock and headed to the house. Now that she was secure, and Bobby was doing his digging, and the target had been eliminated. I could let Arthur know I'd completed the job, and I could get some damn sleep.

CHERISE

I sat on the floor, the cold concrete beneath my thin jeans an endless reminder of how chilled I was. My head leaned back against the wall, and I closed my eyes. There had to be a way out of my mess.

Thinking back to every spy movie I'd watched over the years, I tried to find something that would pertain to my exact situation. Bound and locked away in what offered every indication of being a kill room.

That was my current situation.

I doubted any of the James Bonds had found themselves locked away in a kill room. Or maybe they had. I wished I'd paid more attention instead of just drooling over the character's charisma.

Twisting my hands, I tried again to loosen the tape he'd used to bind me. My teeth still ached from using them in an attempt at breaking through the strong adhesive. Apparently, duct tape did work for everything.

Screaming seemed to be the next logical course of action. Not to get help. I doubted a man who had a kill room stashed in his house would be dumb enough to put the room anywhere near a neighbor's hearing. No, my screams were purely an outlet for my rage.

Appropriately exhausted and with a sore throat, I cradled my head in my fists and sucked in gulps of air. Without any idea of how long I'd been in there or how much longer I'd be locked away, panic bubbled up in my chest. I closed my eyes and counted. I took deep breaths using my abdomen, I did every fucking trick any therapist had ever given me to combat the anxiety ready to claw its way out of me, but not a single thing worked.

I was locked away, bound, and awaiting execution. My breath wouldn't catch properly. Air spiraled in and out of my lungs, but it didn't work; my lungs were broken. The walls started to dance, wavy and seductively, like they were mocking me.

I scrambled up to my feet and paced, counting each step out loud, hoping to bring my heart back to a workable pace.

It wasn't working.

Tears flooded my eyes. I walked along each wall, around and around the room, keeping my eyes focused on my feet, trying and still failing to get my lungs to work. My mind spun, and I stopped in the corner of the room. My gaze landed on the drain.

The perfect room.

A little hose down, and anything that happened in there could be washed away.

I sank back to my ass, my head whirling with panic and lack of air.

The edges of my vision blurred as I sucked in more air, faster, hotter air. Was I even exhaling anymore, or just taking in all the oxygen left in the room?

My body shook, and the racing thoughts in my mind ran harder, faster. I flew my head back with my mouth open, gasping for air, wishing it would catch. Hoping my lungs would start working again.

"Cherise." I heard my name, but I was staring up at the ceiling.

"Cherise." Hands grabbed me, shaking me.

I lowered my chin and saw him staring at me. His eyebrows were knitted together, and that fierce scowl of his was twisted. He looked…concerned.

"I need air," I said.

"There's air, just breathe." His hands moved to my wrists. "Slow breaths, darlin'. Don't gulp." His voice was somber, soft.

I stared at his face then watched him cut through the tape on my wrists. He flipped the blade back into the holder and pocketed it.

I dropped my hands to my sides. He cradled my chin, pushing my gaze to his.

"Slow your breathing." His command was hard, that stoic look back in his eyes. "Do it with me." He exaggerated his inhale, and I followed suit. Slow breath in, and another out. "That's good. Again," he said, his fingers still gripping my chin.

I continued breathing with him, slow in and another out. Finally, my lungs started to work again; my heart followed his rule and slowed down as well.

"There, you're okay now," he said and wiped the hair from my face. I was sweaty and sticky but still so cold. And tired. So much energy wasted on panic. I glanced at the open door. I'd missed an opportunity to run.

"I don't want to die in this room," I said, moving my focus to the drain. "Please don't kill me here."

He frowned. "Come on. Get up." He helped pull me to my feet and pushed back the rest of my hair, tucking it behind my ears. "Let's go." He laced his fingers through mine and led me from the room.

He walked me through the garage, to another door. Hesitant to follow, I slowed.

"It's okay, Cherise," he said and tugged harder. I followed him inside.

It was a house.

Just a house.

He led me up a set of stairs to a bathroom where he pointed to the toilet. I sat on the closed lid and pressed my hands between my knees. Air came easier, and my mind was cleared.

The water in the sink ran, and a washcloth was

handed to me. "Take it." He pushed it at me again.

I pressed it to my face, wiping away the drying sweat and tears. I'd made a mess of myself, which added to the embarrassment and fear I was already experiencing.

"Better?" he asked, taking the cloth from me and laying it on the counter.

I nodded.

"Did you find anything out?" I asked.

"No." He leaned a hip against the counter and crossed his arms over his chest. His glare ran right through me, heating the cold that had set into my bones.

"Do I have to go back to that room?" I asked, lowering my gaze to his chin. I tried to stare at his chest, but the expansive size of it, the strength it represented didn't exactly soothe my nerves.

"You were having an anxiety attack." He avoided

my question with his observation.

"Well, you locked me in a small room meant for—well—" I blinked. This man was a killer. He'd had no hesitation in pulling the trigger and taking down Antonio in the alley. Nothing would stop him from doing the same to me.

I rubbed my jaw. It ached from where he'd punched me, but I hadn't noticed until then how much it hurt.

"I needed you in a quiet spot where you weren't going to get away," he said. "I still do."

"I won't run," I promised.

"I've been promised that before," he said.

I raised my gaze to his. "Not by me."

The side of his lips twitched, like he found me amusing. I was so out of my league with him. I couldn't read his signals. Was he laughing at me or what I said?

"You can stay out of the room, but if you give me any reason—and I mean the slightest reason—you'll go right back in. Anxiety or not. Understand?" He pointed a long finger at me, his jaw tight and his lips thinning as he talked.

I nodded because I wasn't a complete idiot. I'd agree to anything so long as I wasn't being hauled off to be shot and washed down a drainpipe.

"Of course." I finished peeling the duct tape from my wrists and rubbed the sticky skin beneath. I'd have marks for a while.

"You really made a mess of yourself," he said, reaching down and touching the red, raw skin. "All that twisting and pulling irritated it a lot more than the tape did." He tapped my wrist.

"And my jaw? Is that my fault, too?" I couldn't keep the snark from my tone. Now that I was safe from the bad room, a little more backbone showed up.

He shook his head.

"I told you to come; you didn't. When you

don't obey, there're consequences, darlin'." He lifted a shoulder and pushed away from the counter. "You hungry?"

He switched gears too fast for me to keep up with him. But my stomach growled, apparently giving him the answer he wanted.

His gun was still strapped to his side, and, once I caught sight of it, I couldn't let go.

"Do you always carry your gun around your house, or is just because I'm here?" I asked softly. At least it wasn't in his hand anymore. I much preferred it on his hip to having it pointed at my face or touching me.

"Where I go, she goes," he said.

"She? Does she have a name?" I asked, almost finding humor in him. Almost.

His lips quirked. "Simone."

"You named your gun Simone?" I tried to keep my

voice solid, not laugh, but he'd named his gun Simone.

"Everyone has their quirks. I have Simone, you have your shell. How's that working for you? That climb?" His eyebrow arched, and his lips spread into an all-out grin.

I understood the signal this time. He was laughing at me.

"Fuck you," I whispered and lowered my gaze.

He laughed.

"Only if you're real sweet to me." He stepped back to the doorway. "You can stay in the bedroom over here. No leaving, and don't bother with the windows, I have security cameras outside the house. Any movement will alert me. I'd be on you before you hit the ground."

I got up from the toilet and followed him down the hall. "Trading one room for another?" I asked.

"There's windows here you can open." He pushed

the door and revealed the room. "A bathroom's connected, so there's no reason to be walking around the house."

I looked at the doorframe. "There's no lock," I pointed out. I could be free of the room the moment he walked away.

"Not yet. If I have to put one on for you, it's going to be bad first." His eyes narrowed when he spoke, sending a shiver through me. I didn't need further explanation to know what *bad* meant.

I touched my jaw. "Got it."

His eyes lowered. "I'll bring some food up in a bit."

What was the protocol when your kidnapper and could-be murderer offered food?

"'kay," I said lamely. I walked past him, feeling the heat of his body brush mine, and into the bedroom.

The door pulled shut, and the silence crowded

me. Folding my arms over my stomach, I stared at the door. I couldn't get a handle on him.

One minute, he terrified me, convinced me I had limited hours to live. The next, he pulled me out of the death grip of my anxiety and offered me a bedroom suite in his house.

I caught sight of myself in the mirror hanging over a dresser. My hair could double as a squirrel's nest, and my face was marred with smeared mascara. The dark bluish-purple marking on my jaw, thanks to his massive fist, added a bit of color to my otherwise pale complexion.

I sank down onto the plush mattress of the bed. The room had a sweet flavor to it. Decorated with white and light greens, it had the distinct taste of a guest room. But why would a killer like Dustan need a guest room?

Glancing back at the door, I sighed. Who the hell

was I being held captive by, and what was coming next?

More questions than answers. I flicked away a tear that dared to roll down my cheek. Crying hadn't helped so far, and I was too tired to go through another attack. Lying back on the bed, I tucked my knees into my chest and closed my eyes.

The questions would still be there after I woke up, and maybe there'd be a few answers to go with them.

DUSTAN

My office was less of an office and more of a sanctuary. Probably because I spent most of my time while home in there. I had knocked out a wall and made the space large enough for my desk, all my computer shit, and my workout bench.

I wasn't as into working out as some, but it was necessary if I was going to keep up with my line of work. Becoming a member of the Cavalieri hadn't been a hard decision to make. Arthur could be an ass, and I had no idea how he came up with the jobs he assigned, but I didn't care. I'd come to his ranks with my eyes open wide and checked my moral compass at the door.

He said someone needed killing, they got killed.

That was the only moral code I needed to keep myself sleeping soundly at night. I rarely did much background checking into a target other than to make my plans. I didn't need to understand why the target needed eliminating in order to get rid of them. I never asked Bobby to check too deeply into the target, either, just enough for me to know what might pop up at me. I'm sure he preferred it that way. Though I suspected Bobby had other clients he ran intel for who had blacker souls than myself. I never asked, and he didn't offer.

It was a simple arrangement.

And yet, I found myself sitting at my desk, plowing through the Facebook profile of Cherise Styles. Most of the photographs were of her in college. Nothing recent other than some sightseeing pics from around Chicago. She had a thing for museums, apparently.

But other than trips to the beach or walks along

the mag mile, there were no photos of friends or boyfriends. The lack of boyfriends caught my attention first, but I wasn't going to analyze it.

She'd gone to college in Minnesota, but lived in Chicago now? Where was her family?

I lounged back against the soft leather of my chair and tapped the desk with my fingers. Her social media accounts didn't give me any insight as to why the Merde family would want her found. If the cops were looking for her, it wasn't because they wanted answers about Antonio's disappearance. The Merdes had too much pull in the Chicago PD to allow any investigation they didn't want.

I didn't ask Arthur a lot of questions when he assigned me a hit, but when I got the word about Antonio, I wanted info on any retaliation I might see coming. He'd been assuring that there would be none. Antonio's hand had been caught in the family cookie jar, and his disappearance would be seen as a blessing.

Arthur may be lots of things, many of them dark and dirty, but he didn't put us in jeopardy. So, if the Merde family didn't really give a shit about Antonio's death, why were they trying to get their hands on Cherise?

My phone vibrated in my pocket.

Bobby.

"Hey, you have anything for me?" I asked, clicking my screen over to the surveillance camera in Cherise's bedroom.

"Not much. She's boring as fuck, actually," Bobby said. "But I did find out the cops don't give a shit about Antonio. They really only want the girl, and my connection says it's a seize and deliver operation."

"So, the Merde family wants her."

"Yeah. And it's not just the dirty cops looking, they put out a reward. One million is sitting on that girl's head."

My body went rigid.

"A million?"

"Yeah, man. You have a fucking lottery ticket in your hands." The joviality in Bobby's voice put me on edge.

"What do they want her for?" I asked, watching the screen. She was still sleeping. Her hands were tucked neatly between her knees. She hadn't climbed beneath the quilts or even slid her shoes off. Though, after that panic attack, she was probably exhausted.

"Don't know. Does it matter?"

She'd been ready to hyperventilate herself right into passing out when I'd gotten to her in the safe room. I'd seen panic attacks before, knew it for what it was the moment it took her over, but she dove fast. I could have just let her pass out and left her until I figured shit out. It would have been easier. She'd be locked in a safe place where she wouldn't cause any trouble.

Moving her to the spare room meant I needed to watch her more carefully. If the Merde family wanted her, they had reasons. I needed to figure out those reasons.

"Dustan. Does it really matter?" Bobby asked a second time.

"Keep digging and see if you find the connection. Let me know when you do." I clicked off the call, not answering his question and not wanting to dive into that side of the pool just yet.

I logged in and sent off a message to Arthur that the job was complete. I couldn't hold off telling him any longer. He'd probably already seen the media coverage on Antonio's disappearance. I left Cherise out of it, for now.

Once I had more information, I'd clue him in.

He didn't need to know about her anyway. The target had been Antonio, and he was taken care of. If there was another job, he'd send it when it was ready for me. Until then, I needed to figure out my little captive.

One minute, she showed me the fire burning inside of her, the next she tried to hide behind it. If she knew something, would she tell me, or was she keeping it to herself?

Maybe a few more hours in the safe room would get her talking. She'd probably suffer another attack, especially since she seemed to think I'd put her there to kill her, but afterward she might be more pliable.

I flicked my computer screen back over to her room. The bed was empty.

The door to the attached bathroom opened, and she appeared. She ran her fingers through the tangled mess of her shoulder-length dark hair and walked to the window. She pushed the curtains from the window and slipped her fingers through the slats of the blinds, opened them, and looked out.

All she'd see was forest. The house couldn't be seen from any major roads, and the one side road leading to my land was well hidden from the unknowing eye. If someone wasn't looking for it, they'd miss it completely.

I hadn't lied about the sensors around the house. Between the cameras, sensors, and every other security measure I took, if someone so much as sneezed near my property line I knew about it.

Cherise pulled the thin string to raise the blinds then unlatched the window. The alarm sounded on my phone and the computer, but I shut them down. With a hard tug, which was completely unnecessary, she yanked the window upward, stumbling back at the ease of the activity.

I shook my head. Such a dramatic girl.

She still had the screen to contend with, but easily popped it out, angling it and pulling it back inside the room with her. Once it was leaning against the wall, she pressed her hands to the window ledge and leaned outside, looking around the window and down at the ground.

"You won't see the sensors, darlin'. But they're there," I said to her image.

She pulled herself back inside the room and looked around. Picking up a pillow from the bed, she went back to the window.

"What are you doing?" I asked with a smile tugging at my lips.

She dropped the pillow out the window and froze, turning her head slowly as though listening intently.

I chuckled to myself. Did she think sirens would blare to alert her the sensors had been triggered? That pillow wasn't heavy enough to set anything off, but it didn't seem like she knew that.

She looked satisfied with her little experiment and began to climb out the window. My jaw set firm at the sight of her crawling out onto the narrow ledge outside that room. If she slipped and fell, she'd break her fucking neck.

I got up from my chair and opened the app on my phone. I could watch her as I made my way outside to her.

She obviously didn't believe me when I said things would be bad for her if she tried to leave on her own. Or she was momentarily braver than I'd given her credit for.

Either way, Cherise was going to have a very bad afternoon.

CHERISE

I'd completely underestimated the height of the bedroom. Pressing myself against the pale-blue siding, I looked down again at the ground. Much higher than I had originally thought.

But there was a tree. I had to get to it. I worked my way along the narrow ledge toward it, doing my best not to look down again.

As a kid growing up with the woods all around us, I had learned to scramble up and down trees almost as nimbly as any squirrel. The fact that it had been at least a decade since doing such an activity would have to be evaluated at another time. I had to climb down and away from his house. Away from him.

The man named his gun.

Who does that?

A psychopath, that's who. I already knew he was a killer, but adding crazy on top of murderer completely upped the ante.

The short nap I'd taken had re-energized me. The panic attack had been horrible, and embarrassing, but it served me in the end because he'd taken me out of that horrible room and put me in the guest room.

A sharp wind blew through my hair and into my mouth, cutting off my air for a moment. I pressed harder into the house as I came up to the tree. I could do it; I had to do it.

Finding my breath again, I turned away from the wind to inspect the limbs. I needed to jump. That realization sucked some of the air from my lungs, too. If I missed, I'd fall, hitting branches on the way down before finally breaking my face on the ground below.

I took another deep breath and blew out my cheeks as I exhaled. I could do it.

No choice.

Either take my chances here, or go back inside and take my chances with Dustan.

The tree offered better odds.

I blinked a few more times, gauging the space and how hard I would have to push off from the house to make the jump. I'd have to grab onto the trunk right away, wrap my arms around it so I didn't slide down.

Suddenly, my tree climbing experience with didn't feel as extensive. They were old trees back home, with large limbs, and they were low. Much lower than this one. Plus, I'd never actually jumped onto one before. I'd been on the ground first.

I looked back at the window I'd climbed out of. The curtains were blowing out with the wind. I couldn't go back.

Taking a deep breath, I squeezed my eyes closed, reached out, and pushed off from the ledge. I opened my eyes just as the trunk came into view, and I grappled for it. I missed the branch I'd been aiming for and slid down the rough bark. I groaned as my foot finally found a thick branch and stopped the downward fall.

My left cheek burned, and I was sure I'd torn it to pieces with the bark, but I had to keep moving. I worked my way down another branch, until I was at the last one. Another jump, and I was on the ground.

Feet hit first then my knees. I froze, waiting to hear something—anything. An alarm maybe.

What I heard was worse.

The click of a gun being cocked.

"Stand up, Cherise." His cold voice trickled down my spine like melting snowflakes. I lifted my head to survey the distance between where I remained on my knees and the tree line. If I could make it into cover, maybe I'd have a chance at outmaneuvering him through the woods. I hadn't been horrible in track, even if it had been almost a decade since I'd jumped a hurdle.

"You've caused enough trouble for yourself. Don't make it worse." Grass crunched beneath his feet with each step he took toward me.

If I made it to the woods, these were his woods. He probably knew them backward and forward, and who knew if he had traps laid out in them. This wasn't a man I understood, other than when he'd warned me bad things would happen—he meant it.

Pushing off the ground, I rose to my feet and turned to face him. My cheek burned, my knees ached, but neither of those sensations meant anything once I laid eyes on his furious gaze.

A little tic in his jaw gave away the tension, but it was the black fire burning in his eyes that had my breath stuck in my throat. The barrel of the gun pointed at me, again, didn't compare to the ice being shot at me through his gaze.

"What did I tell you would happen if you tried to leave?" he asked, his voice a chilled controlled volume.

"You said it would be bad." I raised my chin a fraction.

"That's right. And do I look like the sort of man who talks to just hear myself?"

"No." I shook my head. His finger was on the trigger, I noticed it and, once I did, I couldn't tear my gaze from it.

"You're a puzzle, Cherise," he said, though it didn't sound anything like a compliment. "You're obviously terrified. I can see you shaking, but yet you climb out of a fucking window and down a goddamn fucking tree!" His voice rose at the end of his sentence, like he was just gearing up for the real anger to hit him.

"I'm more afraid of staying than of going," I said easily. It was the truth, so it wasn't hard to say it, but, looking at him—that was getting harder with each passing moment.

"Well, then I think I need to change that." I uncocked the gun but didn't put it away. "Take off your clothes."

I retreated a step, bringing my arms across my chest. "What? No. Why?"

"I warned you. I told you it would be bad. Now, take them off." Even with the gun no longer an immediate threat, it was still in his hand and I had really stretched my luck already.

I grabbed the arm of my sweater and pulled my arm through then the other and shoved it over my head. Keeping it in front of me, I glanced at him, hoping it had been enough.

His left eyebrow arched pointedly, but he said

nothing. He didn't need to.

I dropped the sweater and shoved out of my jeans, having to first kick off my shoes. Once my jeans were piled on top of my sweater, I checked his expression again. No change.

I wasn't done, apparently.

I kept my eyes closed as I removed my bra and shimmied out of my panties, tossing both onto the pile at my feet. I wrapped my arms over my chest and crossed my ankles to give myself at least some sense of coverage. But when I opened my eyes, I saw him, saw the way his tongue touched his top lip. Saw the cold anger wane into something warmer.

"Turn around and walk back to the tree. Wrap your arms around the trunk." He took another step in my direction, the gun still raised.

Not in any position to argue, and now barefoot, the woods marathon didn't seem such a good idea. I made my way to the tree. The trunk wasn't very thick, and my arms wound around it easily enough.

I heard him shuffling behind me and then step around until he was back in my view. The gun had been replaced with a long black zip tie.

"Wrists together," he commanded but didn't wait for me to move. He grabbed my arms and pulled me forward. My cheek hit the trunk, renewing the ache from my earlier meeting with the bark. The tie wrapped around my wrists and bit into me when he pulled it tight. I tried to jerk back, but he was stronger and had me bound.

"There." He peered at me from around the trunk. "Now the bad time starts."

Starts?

I was already cold and terrified. What was coming next?

He stepped to the side, to where I could see him

plainly and, with precise movements, he unbuckled his thick black leather belt. My heart picked up speed with each loop the strap passed through as he pulled it free of his pants.

"Dustan," I said, but I had no further words. I doubted begging would work. Besides, my mind was too busy engrossing itself in all the horrible things he could do with me tied up the way I was.

"Bad things for bad girls," he said and folded the belt in hand, tucking the metal buckle into his palm.

"Dustan, wait, wait, wait." I was a broken record, without a pause button. But he didn't seem to notice. He made his way back behind me.

I strained my neck, trying to see him, but I couldn't get enough room to twist. I was pressed against the trunk of the goddamn tree.

"No!" I screamed. "Don't you fucking touch me!"

His body pressed against my back. The rough

ridges of the bark bit into my naked flesh, but the heat of his breath on my ear washed away that discomfort.

"Bad things for bad girls," he whispered in that heart wrenchingly controlled voice.

"Please. Please. I'll stay put," I promised as soon as he stepped back again. "I swear." I tried to look over my shoulder again but was cut off by a blindingly sharp pain crossing my ass.

My voice failed me when I tried to scream, but when another lash hit, I found it.

Again, and again, the thick leather slashed my ass, my thighs. I rose up to my toes, screaming out with the burn, the white-hot burn of each strike of his belt.

It wasn't uncontrolled fury ruling his actions. The man was calculated even with his punishments. I kicked out my foot when a lash hit the upturn of my ass.

"Stop! Stop!" I yelled. Trying to twist away only

resulted in the bark pressing into my breasts and thighs. I couldn't get away.

My mind reeled; every coherent thought cut off by another sharp lash of his belt.

"Stop!" I screamed over and over again until my throat felt as stretched and bruised as my ass and thighs. Tears flooded my eyes, running down my cheeks, nearly chocking me with their volume.

My nose ran as I began to sob. I had never in my life experienced such pain, such unadulterated burn as he inflicted on me in silence. He hadn't uttered a word since he began.

"Please! Please!" I cried, pressing my forehead to the tree as another blow hit my thighs. My shoulders ached from being bound, and the more I sobbed, the more my shoulders shook radiating pain throughout my entire body.

He would kill me this way. He didn't need his

gun; he would just beat me until I bled out all over his grass.

The tension in my arms, my back, all released, and I crumpled against the trunk. He wouldn't stop until he was ready. The tears continued to rain down my cheeks. My harsh gasps echoed in my mind, and finally I realized he'd stopped.

"Bad things for bad girls," he said once more, and his fingers traced over my ass. I hissed; the gentleness of his touch stung.

"I'm sorry," I panted, my eyes closed off from seeing him.

"I'm sure you are, darlin'." The ice melted from his voice, and his soft tone was back. But I wasn't stupid enough to believe he would be showing me any real pity or concern.

"But we aren't done, yet." His fingers slipped between my ass cheeks. Instantly, I clenched, but he only laughed at my attempt. The whipping had left me weak, my fighting him wasn't going to be a problem for him.

"No!" My voice cracked. Too much screaming and too much crying.

He wrapped one hand in my hair, pulling my head back against him. His lips brushed my ear.

"Your body is saying something else." He lowered his hand, searching out my sex. Finding me wet and wanting.

I blinked, and more tears fell. "No. Please," I whispered.

"Women react differently to my belt. Some get the punishment and move on, but others…" his fingers slid through my folds, upward toward the tense bundle of nerves that would give me completely away. "Others soften, get wet and ready for me." He pressed hard on my clit. "You're one of those women."

I moaned my humiliation. "It's just a reaction...it means nothing," I said, focusing on the tree branches above me and not wanting to see his smugness.

"Of course," he agreed, running his finger over my clit in circles. "Just a biological reaction." He slid back down my slit and thrust two digits into my pussy. I bit down on my lip. I would not cry out for him. He would not know how good his administrations felt.

"Stop. Please," I said.

He laughed. A deep, throaty chuckle. "You say that, but your ass is pressing against my hand."

I froze. He was right. My back was arched.

"Beg me to make you come," he whispered into my ear.

I shook my head best I could with his hand still holding my hair.

"Beg me, Cherise. Show me you can be a good girl; you can obey me. Because if you can't—if you're still going to be a bad girl...what happens?" His fingers were pumping in and out of me, making straight thinking damn near impossible.

"Bad things," I choked out. My ass still hurt, and the fabric of his pants rubbing against me didn't help. But his fingers, moving in and out of me, stretching me and flicking my clit, those were taking my mind off the pain.

"That's right. Show me you can be good. Beg me." He pressed his body to me, drawing my attention to his erection pushing against my hip. He could take whatever he wanted with the position he had me in. He didn't need me to give permission or even to want it, but he held back.

He didn't want to fuck me. He wasn't done with his lesson, with the bad things. He'd given me pain, and now he was giving me humility.

"We aren't done here until you are a good girl," he

said, flicking my clit harder.

"Please," I whispered, feeling a tear trickle down my cheek and into my hairline.

"Please what?" he whispered, taking my earlobe between his teeth.

"Please make me come for you." The words shook, but he heard them.

"There's a good girl." He thrust another digit into me, biting harder on my earlobe.

I moaned, arching back at him. He let go of my hair and slipped his free hand between me and the tree. He found my clit easily and worked it in circles while fucking me harder and harder with his fingers.

"When you're ready, you come hard," he commanded, running his tongue over the shell of my ear.

The pressure built and built.

"You can do this. You can be a good girl." His

words came just as the dam broke, and I cried out with more fury, hard waves rocking through my core. My thighs shook with the rest of my body as my orgasm peaked and sent me plummeting back down to reality.

My erotic pants of pleasure morphed into soft sobs full of humiliation and pain. The throbbing of my pussy paled in comparison to the hot pulsing ache of my ass and thighs. With the arousal gone, all the pain came forward.

His hands slipped from between my legs, and he made his way back around the tree. I had my head against the trunk but felt the cool blade of a knife slip between my wrists and slice through the plastic tie. My arms swung down to my sides, and I had to catch myself before I slumped down to the ground.

His hands came back, and he lifted me. I didn't struggle. What would be the point? He'd already showed me he had more control over my body than

I did.

Bad things happen to bad girls. He'd said that more than once, and I had all the proof in my sore muscles and bruised pride to believe him.

He carried me through the house and up a set of stairs, but I was staring at the stubble on his chin too hard to pay attention to the layout of the place. Escape wouldn't happen. Not with Dustan watching me.

He brought me inside another bedroom and kicked the door shut. Gently, he laid me on the bed and threw a blanket over me.

"Your cheek is cut up from that fucking tree." He touched the wounds, making me flinch. "I'll have to clean it."

I didn't answer. Would anything I said matter anyway?

DUSTAN

Cherise appeared in the kitchen doorway the next morning wearing one of my white button-down shirts. It was too big for her smaller frame. The hem hit just below the ass, and she had the sleeves rolled up to her elbows. Her hair was still damp from her shower, the tips of her locks brushing wet streaks across the shoulders of the material.

"I made you some coffee." I pushed a cup across the kitchen island toward her. Even with a full night's sleep, she still looked like hell. That damn tree she'd slid down had scraped her cheek, adding to the bruise I'd given her when I had to get her out of her apartment in a hurry. She raised her hand to push her hair back behind her ear and exposed the purple circles around her wrist. The duct tape had made her skin sensitive, but the zip ties had dug deeper into her flesh.

"Do you have creamer and sugar?" she asked, eyeing the fridge.

I nodded. "In there."

She grabbed the small carton and poured enough into the cup to turn the perfectly good coffee into a fucking milkshake. I watched with fascination as she scooped three heaping spoons of sugar into the cup before finally giving it a stir.

"What?" she asked when she noticed me gawking.

I hid my smile behind my own sip of coffee. "Nothing."

She put the creamer away and leaned a hip against the counter.

"There's a chair if you want." I pointed to the stool within her reach.

She shook her head and sipped her coffee.

"How's your ass?" I put my cup down and slid around the island, cutting off her escape route and getting closer to her.

"Fine." Her eyes didn't meet mine though. She was staring at my chin again.

"Hmm." I rubbed my jaw. "Let me see."

Her gaze shot up to mine. "Why?"

"So, I can check for any cuts or bruises." I twirled my finger in the air. "You're not going to be a bad girl again so soon, are you?" It was a cheap shot, threatening her with more whippings for not showing me her ass, but it got her moving.

She huffed, but she obeyed. She put her cup down, hard enough to splash a bit over the side, and spun around, shoving her ass at me. The whipping hadn't scared off her fierceness.

Good.

I hooked the hem of the shirt with my thumb and pulled it upward, over her ass. Several of the lashes had left a dark-purple bruise, but there were only two welts. No broken skin. I'd controlled my strength better than I'd thought. Every time I pulled my belt back, I imagined her falling headfirst from the fucking tree. She could have, no, she would have, broken her goddamn neck.

The fact that her self-endangerment pissed me off more than her escape attempt didn't get past me, but I wasn't in the mood to entertain it. She'd disobeyed, she'd put herself at fucking risk, and she'd been punished for it. If she did it again, I'd do it all over again.

I lightly traced one of the welts. My dick lengthened in my pants, pressing against the zipper when she hissed. Fuck, such a sweet sound.

"Do you want your panties?" I asked, still touching

her.

She stilled. Her chin rose when she turned to look back at me. "Maybe later," she said softly.

I grinned at her. "I'm sure those lovely purple underpants won't hurt too much."

Her cheeks reddened, and she yanked her body away from me. She stepped around the island, taking her coffee cup with her.

"I wasn't expecting—" she cut off her own explanation. "I don't owe you anything."

I raised my eyebrows. "True enough. You don't." I grabbed my cup and rinsed it out before dumping it into the dishwasher. "It's cute though," I said, shutting the door.

"Cute?"

"Yeah. Most women have all sorts of lacey things or wear those floss panties. It's cute that you wear those."

"You think my granny panties are cute?" She held her cup to her lips, like my statement had shocked her into a freeze frame.

"Yeah." I nodded with a laugh. "I'd prefer no panties at all." I moved closer to her again, drawn to her while her guard was slipping. "Ever."

"You're crazy."

"I've been called worse," I admitted sliding up to her and placing my hand on her hip.

Her smile faded into concern. "Have you figured out anything?"

My jaw clenched, but I forced it to relax. I had sent all the information I had to Arthur, and I was waiting for his response. If he put a price on her head, then I had a job to do. I preferred to wait to think about it until his answer came through.

"Why were you at the bar that night?" I asked, splaying my fingers across her hip.

Her muscles tensed; her eyes lowered to my chest.

"It was stupid." She rolled her eyes. "I mean really stupid, right? Look what happened." She huffed a laugh, like she was doing her best to find humor in the situation. If she knew what was going on behind the scenes, she wouldn't be smiling so brilliantly at me.

"That book?" I asked, remembering the self-help book sitting on her nightstand. "The one that's supposed to help think outside the box?"

"Climb out of my shell," she corrected me and placed her cup back on the counter with a sigh.

"Ah, yeah. So, let me ask you this. Why me? When you walked into that bar, you came over to me. Why?" I didn't exactly have a welcoming aura around me—I'd been told.

Her blush crept up her neck, taking over her cheeks and her nose. She tried to turn away, but I caught her chin between my fingers and pulled her face back.

"Tell me." I lowered my voice, knowing she'd react to the dominance laced in my tone.

She sighed. "It's stupid."

"Tell me anyway."

She waited a beat. "You were safe."

Surprise washed through me. "Safe?"

"Completely out of my league. I knew nothing would come of it, so it wouldn't hurt. It was just practice," she rambled.

"What do you mean, practice?" The surge of protectiveness blossoming inside me wasn't making my mood lighter.

"I mean, you looked preoccupied. So, I figured you weren't there to hook up. Unlike the other guys there."

"That doesn't answer my question." I pressed my body into her hip, liking the sensation of her body against mine.

"I was flirting," she blurted out. "I was practicing what the book suggested."

"The book suggested you down a few drinks and ramble to a perfect stranger?" The author was probably a fucking jackass looking for new ways to screw insecure women.

"Does it really matter?" She glanced up and I caught sight of the insecurity, the vulnerability lying right in front of me, raw and untamed. This girl wasn't a danger to anyone but herself.

"You don't have friends to go to bars with you?" I showed a little mercy, giving her a bit of space from the topic she obviously would rather not discuss.

"No. Not really. I've only lived in Chicago for a year."

"A year's a long time." I pushed her hair back again when it fell forward over her face.

"Not when you don't know anyone." She blew out

a long breath, puffing up her cheeks.

"Where'd you live before?" I asked, driven by curiosity and longing to know more about her than just how fucking gorgeous she was without clothes on, or how delicious she sounded when she orgasmed.

"Are you going to hurt me?" She turned the question on me so fast, I had to take a moment to let the change in topic sink in.

"Haven't you heard that it's in your best interest to humanize yourself to your attacker?" I gripped her hip, letting my fingers dig into her curves.

"Have people tried that with you?" she asked softly, looking up at me through her lowered lashes.

"Yes." I wouldn't lie to her. Lying made things complicated, and, in my experience, complications were easily acquired without adding to them.

"And did it work?"

"No." I moved around her, hooking my hand

around her other hip and pulling her toward me.

A job was a job. I didn't need details, and I didn't want any. If a target got chatty, I shut that shit down. Maybe that made me less human, more of a monster, but one thing I never did was give hope where there was none. I didn't pretend there was another option. There was a goal, I had a job, and it got done. Period.

"Where'd you live before Chicago?" I asked again, running my fingers up from her hip around to her ass. She grimaced when I touched the welts. A little reminder of the effects of disobedience.

"A farm town in Minnesota. Tiny little town."

"And what you'd do there?"

"Dreamt about leaving," she deadpanned.

I laughed. "Okay, so little farm girl leaves for the big city. What about college?"

"I went."

I let go of her ass and ran my fingers across her

cheek, inspecting the scrapes for any sign of infection. She'd gotten lucky with that damn tree.

"And?"

"And what?"

"Okay, family. What about your parents?" I pushed on. Getting to know her was a bad idea. Arthur could message me any minute, and she'd be less of a curiosity and more of a target. I was walking a tightrope with her, but I couldn't seem to stop myself.

"They died in a house fire when I was away at college." Her voice dipped, but she didn't pull away from my touch. My gaze wandered to hers, searching her for the truth.

"The farm?" I pressed.

"It's still there." She swallowed. "My uncle runs it now."

A chill ran through my veins. "What kind of farm?"

She blinked and inhaled deeply. "Flowers. I think. I'm not sure."

"You're not sure?" I pulled back and studied her. "How do you not know what your family grows?"

She lifted her shoulders. "My dad grew mostly soybeans, but he had a small plot for poppy flowers—you know, for the seeds, but my uncle changed it when he took over. I think it's all flowers now."

I ran my thumb over her lips. The topic needed to change. I didn't want to go digging and find something I had to address.

"Your uncle and you close?"

"No," she said with finality. The word came out hard, and she wouldn't look at me.

"Not a nice guy?"

"He's a prick," she said.

"He hurt you?" I didn't need to hear her say it, I already knew. I could sense it on her when she mentioned him, when I asked about him. The tension grew, and fear edged its way into her eyes. "Why does he have the farm and not you?" I asked, letting her have another reprieve.

"My dad left it to him." She blinked, but I could see the confusion lurking there. "I'm not sure really how it all happened."

Cradling her face in my hands, I tilted her head back. "You were wrong at the bar. I'm not out of your league." My thumb brushed her lip again. So full, so fucking kissable. "And you had every fucking chance of turning my head."

Her tongue slipped out between her lips, wetting them for me, inviting me. And I wasn't saying no. Not to that.

I brushed my lips across hers at first, coaxing a reaction. Her hands came up and flattened against my chest, but she wasn't pushing.

"You shouldn't have gone out in that alley, darlin'. But I'm not entirely sure I wish you hadn't." I didn't give her a chance to answer or to let my words seep into her mind. Crushing my lips to hers, I possessed her, claimed her.

Her lips parted, and I swept in, taking the kiss deeper, owning another piece of her and wanting even more. Her fingers curled into my chest, but still she didn't push me away. She tasted like honey, but better, so much fucking better.

I pressed my body against hers, feeling every bit of her tension and letting her feel every inch of my cock. I wanted her, needed to get inside her, and the reasons for these desires could be examined later. All I knew was my body was reacting to her more than it had ever done with a woman before.

Her breaths came out in short bursts when I pulled back from her, kissing the tip of her nose before backing off. Fucking her in my kitchen wasn't exactly a smart thing to do, and I needed to get that damn message from Arthur before I messed everything up.

"There's food in the fridge. Get something to eat." I stepped back, denying myself her touch. "I'll get some ointment for your scratches. You should put some antibiotic stuff on it." I touched the red marks on her cheek.

"Okay," she said softly, her hands gripping the counter behind her.

"Okay." I gave a curt nod and left her in the kitchen.

My phone buzzed, and I swiped angrily across the screen to open the conversation.

Arthur's orders came through.

CHERISE

After filling myself with a ham sandwich, I went upstairs and dressed. Dustan had left my clothes neatly folded on the bed. I did a quick survey of my backside before slipping into the panties and jeans. The dark marks across my ass cheeks and a few lingering on my thighs were tender, but the clothing didn't bother them too much.

I looked out the bedroom window at the forest still in view. He'd accomplished his goal with that whipping. I was definitely more worried about what would happen if I tried to leave than if I stayed. Because it wasn't a matter of if I was caught, just when. Dustan had known exactly where I was before I even touched the ground. He'd find me, and I didn't want to think about what would happen after that.

Instead, I decided to do some recon of my own. I checked out his bedroom. Full-on masculine with sharp-edged furniture, dark-stained woods and deep blues for the fabrics. A drastic contrast to the guest room he had me in at first.

I couldn't stay in the bedroom forever. There weren't even any books to read. Leaving it behind, I explored the rest of the house. The same cold atmosphere in every room.

"What are you doing?" His hard tone startled me as I turned a doorknob.

I lifted a shoulder. "Looking around."

His eyebrows rose. Maybe he wasn't used to honesty from people around him. I didn't need a full job description to understand what he did to pay for the house I was standing in. The man lived with a gun on his hip. A gun he'd named.

"For a way out?" He crossed his arms over his chest. He would look a little less formidable if he'd wear something more casual than the white button-downs. The crisp creases of his slacks added to his all-business appearance.

"I already found the doors," I said softly. I couldn't gauge him yet. There was tension in his body language, in his set jaw, but his eyes had warmed.

"But you didn't open them?"

"No." I couldn't hide the exasperation from my tone. "I was bored. And sitting there just thinking about all the ways you could kill me and wondering why you haven't done it yet, and then trying to guess when you would finally do it—" I paused a beat. "I needed a break from the worry."

He frowned. "You worry a lot."

"You have a gun that you keep pointing at me!

Look at my face." I pointed at myself. "You punched me, you whipped me..." And then he kissed me, but I didn't mention that joy of a memory. I didn't know what that was, or if it meant anything in terms of my future as a living human being, but I wasn't going there with him. For all I knew, he was just enjoying himself—toying with his prey. Like a cat bats around a mouse before finally doing it in. I could be the mouse.

"All of that's true." He nodded. "But I don't recall ever telling you I was going to kill you." He dropped his hands to his hips, hooking them there. The top of his shirt opened with his movements, showing off a bit of his chest. I could make out a patch of dark hair. Not overgrown like some wooly mammoth, but enough to make my fingers itch to touch.

I clenched my jaw and forced my gaze up to his chin. Not that the neatly trimmed stubble there didn't make him less appealing, but I needed to put my eyes somewhere that didn't make him look so damn attractive. Dustan wasn't someone to be drooled over. He was something to be feared.

So why couldn't I conjure up the initial terror I'd felt the first time he'd drawn his weapon on me?

"You didn't need to spell it out for me." I gave a pointed look at his gun still hugging his hip. I wondered if he slept with it, too.

His eyes narrowed a fraction. "You get mouthy when you're scared. Forced bravado."

"I can't help it," I muttered, sliding my hands into the back pockets of my jeans. My fingers brushed a welt, but I managed not to groan at the tenderness.

"You surprise me is all," he said. "Not many people do anymore."

I didn't know how to respond to that, so I didn't. He wasn't shuffling me into that horror room or back into the bedroom, so I wasn't ready to push him too hard.

"It's getting late, but I want to show you something." He motioned for me to follow him then walked off down the hall. I let him lead me to his office.

The space was huge and had everything he could need other than a kitchen.

"Do you live in here?" I asked, noticing the television set up with the plush furniture.

He chuckled. "It feels like that sometimes." He walked to his desk and flicked on a monitor. He had several.

No wonder he'd known I was out of the bedroom before I got to the tree. He had cameras all over the house. He clicked a few buttons on a keyboard and the security footage switched over to survey maps.

"That's home," I whispered with surprise and moved closer to the screen. I touched the monitor.

"Here. This is the farm."

"Right. Have you been here?" He tapped a large green space north of the house.

I shook my head. "No. I wasn't allowed outside our property. No one lived over there as far as I know though. Here's the tree line. It ends the property." I pointed out the wooded area that cut off my childhood home from the neighboring plots.

"It doesn't." He scrolled the picture outward more. "See, this is all part of the same property. Your father's property. Land that is still yours," he said, dragging his finger over the dark-blue line on the map.

"That can't be right." I stood up and retreated a step. "After the funerals, the lawyers said the land rolled over to my uncle. I signed papers stating I wouldn't contest it. My uncle set up a fund for me, enough to finish college and then some so that I would go away."

"And you did? No questions asked?" he asked. I

couldn't expect him to understand. A man like him probably never understood the pain of losing someone he loved. If he did, how could he do the things he did? Nor could he understand fear. True fear.

"I was—my uncle made it clear I didn't have much choice." I backed away from Dustan, away from the computer. None of that was my business anymore. It never really was.

"You had choices, you just didn't have anyone there to explain them to you," he said. "Your father. Did he ever try talking to you about business?"

"No." I shook my head. "He wanted me to go to college to get a degree. He didn't want me working the farm."

"He never mentioned what would happen when he retired, or when he died?" Dustan pushed.

"No." I pressed my hand to my throat. I knew how naive I'd been growing up. I didn't need the reminder.

"He just said I wouldn't have to worry about it. He said he'd probably sell it all off before it became an issue."

"And your mom?"

"She didn't like talking about business. She said her job was to manage the house, and Dad's job was to manage the business."

"Pretty old school," Dustan said with a soft laugh at the end.

"I thought that, too. I thought she was just old-fashioned, but she wasn't. She liked to put on blinders when there was something she didn't want to deal with. I figured she was doing the same with the farm. She didn't get involved because she didn't like it."

The little tic in Dustan's jaw appeared. "How often did she put these blinders on when it came to you?"

I cleared my throat. "Dad let me help in the fields

sometimes. But not like other kids. While all the kids at school had been up with the sunrise helping with chores—I didn't have a clue what most of them did. Dad had a small crew, three guys who helped in the fields, but I wasn't allowed to talk to them."

"Sounds like you had your own set of blinders," he said.

"It was better that way." I looked back at the monitor. "You said I still own the land?"

His jaw softened. "Public records still have you listed as the owner."

"How can that be? Uncle Randy showed me the papers."

"I don't know what that was, but it wasn't ownership. That land still belongs to you." He pointed to the screen.

I sighed. "What does this have to do with anything anyway?" I glanced at the windows. The sun had gone down, night arrived with it. Even after the nap, I was tired. I just wanted to sleep away the mess.

"That's what I'm trying to find out." He clicked the button on the monitor, blackening the screen.

"You're not going to let me go, are you?" I asked, feeling the familiar heaviness of defeat push down on my shoulders.

"No. I'm not." The words came out fierce, like he was making a vow, not just answering a question.

"If that land really is mine, that means I'm worth something." I wrapped my arms around my middle. "You can use me to get the land, or money. Something like that?"

"Yeah, I could."

"And the Antonio thing?" I bit the inside of my cheek. He hadn't brought it up, and my years of ignorance showed by jumping the hurdle ahead of him.

"Not really a thing anymore," he said.

"The police aren't looking for me?" I asked, surprised they'd given up so easily.

"They're being handled." His answers weren't assuring me of anything positive. Everything was being buried. That didn't mean I was safe. Just untraceable.

"I don't understand." I shook my head. "If the Antonio thing isn't a thing. If the cops are being dealt with, why the hell am I still here? Why won't you let me go?" I fisted my hands.

He stalked toward me, and I retreated until my back hit a wall. I could read him well enough now. He didn't hide his thoughts. His jaw clenched, his eyes narrowed, but his mouth wasn't tense. His lips were parted, like they were getting ready to say something.

"I have my orders," he said, as though that meant anything to me at all.

"I'm a loose end." My words cracked as they

escaped my drying throat. Electric warnings shot through my body. He'd do it now. He'd end the whole mess with one shot.

"You were." He nodded, caging me with his hands pressed to the wall on either side of my head. "You aren't now."

I swallowed, trying to find words, something that would make him change his mind. I had nothing of real value to offer. If finding out about the farm didn't work, what else could I give him?

"Please don't take me back to that room," I whispered, pissed at the fear shaking in my voice. "It might ruin your carpet, but if it's all the same to you, just do it here?"

His eyes narrowed farther; his face came closer to me. I felt his breath hit my face, smelled his aftershave—musky and sweet.

"You still think I'm going to kill you?"

"You said you won't let me go, and you have orders," I reminded him.

"Correct on both accounts."

His right hand left the wall and cupped my cheek. His thumb ran along the edge of my jaw. The bruise he'd given me still tender, I held back any indication his touch hurt.

"Do you want me to beg you?" I hardened my resolve. I couldn't be the weak little girl who needed self-help books just to go out into the world anymore. I had to do this on my own. No one else would champion for me. "I won't."

He laughed, a low growly sound from deep in his chest. "Oh, you will, darlin'. But not for your life. You won't have to do that." He touched my lips with his finger. "No more questions. I'm not going to hurt you—unless you give me reason. You are still going to obey me, everything I say, but you aren't a target. You aren't in danger with me."

I swallowed back every question wanting to leap from my chest. Relief hit me when I understood his words. I wasn't going to die. He wouldn't kill me—or hurt me.

"You're going to stay with me for as long as it takes to figure out your connection to the Merde family and settle that score. Once that's done, we'll figure out what you're going to do next."

"You're protecting me?" I asked against his finger. Shock replaced my relief.

"I'm protecting important assets, and right now you're one of them." He pressed his lips against my cheek, against the scrapes. "So, no more hurting yourself, darlin', or you'll get more than just my belt."

I could agree to that. I'd had enough scrapes and bruises to last awhile—no need to push my luck.

"Okay,"

"The rules are different now. You're under my protection. Under my complete rule." He kissed my other cheek.

I nodded because no sounds would come out of me, none that didn't begin with a moan and end with a plea for his touch. Maybe it was the relief at not being shot, or the sexy scent of his aftershave, or it could have simply been the heady drawl of his voice as he promised to protect me, but every fiber in my body lit on fire. The need to save my life quickly morphed into a desire to be consumed by him.

"Rule number one. You sleep in my bed." He pulled back, making a show of checking his watch. "And it's bedtime now."

DUSTAN

The slamming of a door jarred me from my focus on my computer. I checked the time. Noon. Cherise was wondering around again.

I left her to her search and went back to scrolling through the maps. Bobby hadn't come through with anything tangible yet, and while I was waiting on him, I decided to do a little digging on my own. I'd been able to find the family farm Cherise mentioned, and the estate lines, but what I couldn't get to was any real information on what the farm actually dealt with.

I knew her uncle was key to this. He had a connection to Merde. I just needed to figure out what that connection was. Arthur wouldn't authorize a move on him until I had a solid lead.

Arthur not calling for Cherise's death surprised me, but, worse, it relieved me. Ten years I'd worked beneath him, and not once did I question his motives or his decisions. He gave a target, and I went to work. But, this time, with her—I wasn't sure I would have been able to complete the job so easily.

Fuck.

Or at all.

For the first time in ten years, the thought of going against Arthur's word danced through my mind. And it was over a girl.

But I didn't have to evaluate it now that Arthur had given the command to investigate her uncle. If there was a target, it wouldn't be Cherise. I could breathe a little easier and get my head back in my work. Taking down a target.

"Dustan." Cherise's voice pulled me from my

research. I leaned to the left and took her in from behind my computer screen.

She'd slept in my shirt. Right beside me. I had felt the heat of her body filling the space between us in my bed. I'd been a fucking gentleman and let her sleep with her panties on, and I didn't touch her.

But, now, she was back in her jeans and sweatshirt. She needed a change of clothes.

Her hair was pulled back into a high ponytail, giving her such an innocent look, I wanted to dive over my desk and begin her corruption.

"Yeah?" I asked, forcing myself to remain casual. Those jeans were hugging her hips the way I wanted to, but I needed to distract myself from that fact.

"I want to go outside, and I don't want you chasing after me with Simone." She folded her arms over her stomach, a little defense she put up between us.

I touched my gun at my hip and grinned. She'd

remembered her name.

"Why do you want to go outside?" I asked, glancing out the window. The sun hid behind clouds, and I could make out the wind blowing through the leaves. "It's crap outside."

"It's boring as hell inside," she shot back at me, with her chin raised. She really did surprise me.

"If you want something from me, I wouldn't advise your attitude make an appearance." I sighed and went back to reading my monitor.

"I'm going out back," she announced. Some of the snark was gone this time.

"Don't go near the tree line." I leaned to the side again. "And get a sweatshirt from my closet. It's cold today."

She stared at me for a long moment. What was there to decide? I'd given her what she wanted.

"Okay." She turned and left me to my work.

I shook my head. I couldn't get a good read on her, which pissed me off more than interested me.

Her footsteps faded up the stairs and, a few minutes later, she came back down. A flash of blue passed my doorway just before the back door opened and shut. At least she'd put on another sweatshirt.

My phone buzzed a few times, and I read over the messages. Bobby didn't have information on Cherise's uncle, but he had some about the Merde family. They were upping the reward for Cherise's capture.

I gave a clear-cut reply of no and slid my phone back onto the desk. I wasn't turning her over to the fucking Merde family for any amount of money. Arthur's orders were to keep her close and dig around about the Styles' family farm. He had suspicions, but he didn't share them with me.

I stood and walked to the window. Cherise was making her way over the grass, straight for the tree line. My jaw clenched. She just couldn't listen to a simple fucking order.

Something startled her. She paused and looked around her, searching out a sound maybe. The wind picked up, blowing loose strands of her hair around her face. She pulled the hoodie tighter around her and started walking again.

The hairs on my neck danced to attention, and I flicked my gaze to her left, off in the distance. Movement in the trees.

Fuck.

With Simone in hand, I ran out of my office, through the house, and burst out into the back yard.

"Cherise!" I screamed for her, but the wind stole my warning and carried it away. She continued walking forward, the hood now pulled up around her ears.

"Fuck! Cherise!" I broke into a full run, weapon ready, toward her while scanning the perimeter. More movement, but I couldn't make out a clear target.

"Cherise!" I yelled again, and this time she heard me. She paused and turned around, her mouth dropping open when she took notice of my gun.

A shot rang out, but not from me.

I waved at her. "Down! Get down!"

She froze for a moment but then dropped to the grass. I ran toward the sound of the shot.

The intruder stepped deeper into a bush, but I'd seen him. I stopped short of the tree line, aiming at his location, and waited.

"Dustan," Cherise called out, but I ignored her.

To the left of the bush, the asshole moved, his arm extended. I fired.

A pained scream followed by the thud of his gun hitting the ground signaled I'd hit him.

"Stay there!" I pointed back at Cherise and ran to finish this.

I found him, a young asshole lying on the ground, holding his arm. I kicked him and rolled him to his back, pressing my foot into his neck.

"Who the fuck sent you?" I asked.

He pushed against my boot, but with an injured arm, and my weight on him, he didn't have much of a chance at success.

"Who?" I urged again, pressing harder into his throat.

"Just need the girl," he choked out, wincing.

I cocked the gun.

"Merde?" I asked, taking aim.

His eyes widened, and his feet scrambled to find purchase on the ground, but he wasn't going anywhere. He struggled, trying to get up from where I had him pinned.

"Yes!" He twisted, but there was no hope.

"How'd you find this location?" I asked. My

house was safe. It wasn't on any map or register. Fuck, even the property tax bill had the wrong address on it. I wasn't findable.

"Fuck you," he spat at me.

The corner of my lips kicked up. Maybe he thought holding back the information would keep him alive. Give him a chance to find a way out of it if I took the time to interrogate him.

He was wrong.

I squeezed the trigger, sending a clean shot through this forehead then stepped away from him, letting the blood pool out onto the forest floor, collecting in the loose leaves and twigs.

A snap of wood behind me signaled Cherise's arrival. I dropped my hand to the side and faced her.

"I told you to stay put." I shoved my gun back in its place.

"Who was he?" she asked, fingertips touching her

lips. The color faded from her cheeks.

"A bad guy," I said and walked over to her. I brushed the loose hairs from her face. "You okay?" I checked her over. That pot shot he took had been aimed at me, but I needed to be sure she was untouched.

Her gaze flicked from the dead asshole on the ground to me. I'd seen fear in those beautiful eyes of hers the first time she'd seen me kill, but this time, there was none. This time, she simply looked curious.

"He was here for you?" she asked, though I could hear the doubt in her voice. She knew.

"No, darlin'. He was here for you."

"Why?" she whispered.

"Like I said, you're an asset." I ran my thumb over her chin. "I told you to stay away from the tree line."

Her eyes narrowed, and her forehead wrinkled.

"You're blaming me?"

I grinned. "No. Just don't want any confusion as

to why you're getting your ass spanked later." I dropped my hand from her face and grabbed hers. "We have to go. But later..." I let the warning fade and tugged her toward the house.

"Leave? For where?" She preoccupied herself with questions, probably thinking I was just blowing smoke about disciplining her later. I wasn't speaking just to hear myself. If she'd made it to the tree line before I'd spotted her, she'd be gone now. That asshole would have had her pulled away through the trees and, no matter how much she screamed, it would have been unlikely that I would have heard her.

Whoever sent the asshole might have followed up with more men, and I wasn't taking chances. I dragged her to my office.

"Stand there." I pointed a finger. "Don't fucking move."

"I don't understand, Dustan. Where else would

we go?" She pulled the sleeves of the sweatshirt down over her hands and tucked her arms in her armpits. The chill from outside had followed us inside, or she was getting scared.

I threw open the doors to the cabinet in the corner of my office and grabbed a bag, filling it with everything I needed. I snagged another bag, pre-packed for situations like this, and slammed the cabinet shut.

"Let's go. Don't talk right now." I grabbed her arm and pulled her along with me to the garage.

She yanked back.

"C'mon, Cherise. You're not going in that room. I promise." I slowed down but kept pulling her with me.

She didn't fight me the rest of the way, but I could see from the corner of my eye that she glared at the door leading to the small room. I'd interrogated more men in that room than I could remember. Most of them met their end in there as well. But it had never been intended for that with her.

I let her hand go and dropped my bags once we reached my car. Pulling off the thick covering, I unveiled my mustang.

"That's your car?" she asked with understandable appreciation.

"It's faster than the sedan," I said, picking up the bags. "Right now, I need speed, not to blend in with working-class bar patrons."

"Where are we going?" she asked again once I climbed into the driver's side.

"Away from here." I threw the car into gear and, the moment the garage door gave enough clearance, we were gone.

CHERISE

We drove for hours before Dustan pulled the car off the highway. I'd asked once too many times about our destination, so he wasn't talking to me at all anymore. The gag lying on the dashboard in front of me was a constant reminder of his last words.

"Another word, darlin', and I'll take care of it for you." He had slammed the ball gag onto the dash. My next question was going to be, who the hell kept a ball gag in his glove compartment, but I had kept it to myself.

"You're hungry," he stated after my stomach made a loud gurgling sound. I'd skipped breakfast earlier, but I wasn't going to mention it. The gag still glared at me.

"You can talk now, darlin'." He laughed softly. "If I'd known you were so against that gag, I would have had it out from the get-go."

"Maybe it's best I just sit here then and let you drive me halfway across the country to whatever destination you feel like taking me. And then maybe I should just follow every order you give me without complaint or question." I kept my gaze fixed on the scenery outside my window.

His hand landed on my thigh, right above my knee, and he gripped hard.

"Yes—to both of those things." He gave my knee a squeeze and let loose a low chuckle. "But I doubt you could do either of them."

"You'll have to excuse my rudeness. I'm not used to people trying to kidnap or kill me." I pressed my forehead to the chilled window. "I suppose I should be used to it by now, seeing as it's happened twice now in the span of two days. Now, people are trying to kidnap me from my kidnapper." I laughed, tossing my head back, feeling the bubble of insanity building inside me. "I mean, seriously, that's funny, right? You steal me from my apartment then this guy shows up trying to steal me from you. And for what?"

I twisted beneath the seat belt to face him.

"I'm a medical receptionist. That's it. I have no money, no power, I have nothing and am nothing. Why the hell would anyone want me? Why would I be an asset to anyone?"

His dark gaze struck me just before he turned the wheel and sped us to the side of the road. Dirt kicked up around the car at the abrupt stop. He threw the gears into park, undid his seat belt, and turned to me. One hand grabbed my headrest while the other pointed at me.

"Two things, darlin'." His calm tone contrasted the heat in his expression, the tension in his mouth and darkness of his eyes. "One, you aren't nothing. Two, you definitely are an asset. Three, say otherwise and I won't be waiting until we get settled for the night before I tan your ass. I'll do it right here on the side of the road."

My breath escaped me. Left me completely alone and, as I tried to find it again, his hand snaked around my neck, pulling me close to him.

He was shaken. Something I'd said had gotten to him. An offhand comment about my worth. This man had slain two men before me without so much as a blink, but I made one stupid remark and he got rattled?

"That was three things," I whispered when it became evident, he wasn't going to say anything more.

He tilted his chin back, his eyes searching my face.

"What?"

"You first said two things, but then you said three," I pointed out softly.

His lips spread out into a gentle grin. "I suppose I did."

"I am sort of hungry," I said, sinking into the warmth of his hand against my neck.

"I heard." He glanced down at my stomach. "We'll grab some food then get back on the road. We have another five hours before we stop for the night."

"You going to tell me where we're going?" I asked, hoping he'd relent in his stubborn stance of keeping it from me.

"Not a chance." He winked and let me go. "There's a town coming up in about twenty minutes. We'll grab food there."

I watched him settle himself back in his seat. "Okay, sure."

The town he took us to had a diner right off the highway exit. A small place that smelled of pancakes and syrup. He led me to a corner booth and slid in across from me.

He clamped his hand down over my menu when I started to open it. "Just get the burger. Trust me." I looked down at the oversized laminated page and nodded.

"Sure. Sounds good." It sounded like heaven, but I was trying to keep my tone casual. Go with the flow. Maybe if I kept more of my questions to myself, he'd start talking. Maybe if I pushed, he'd only pull back.

"Good." He raised a hand, gesturing for the waitress.

An older woman stopped at our table to take our order. Her hair was bound up in a bun. She wore deep-red lipstick that stood out against her pale complexion.

"And to drink?" she asked as she scribbled the

double order of burgers onto her pad.

"Diet—"

"Two root beers," he said over me.

She paused in her scribbling and glanced between us.

"How do you know I'm not diabetic?" I asked.

He ignored me and looked up at the waitress. "Two root beers, and extra fries on her plate." He pointed a long finger at me but still hadn't looked in my direction.

The waitress's lips twisted up on the right side, and she made her notes.

"You got it." She tucked the pad back into her apron and collected the menus from us. "A man wants you to have extra fries, he's a keeper." She winked at me and walked off toward the kitchen with our order.

Dustan chuckled.

"Seriously?" I jerked a thumb toward the retreating

waitress. "What if I don't like root beer?"

He shrugged. "You'll survive."

I blinked. "So, you don't care." What a stupid argument to have with the man who'd abducted me, whipped me, and was only a few hours away from trying to give me another punishment.

"About your pop choice? No. Not really." He drummed his fingers on the table. "You aren't diabetic, by the way. If you were, we'd probably already have had an issue on our hands by now. You haven't exactly been eating routinely, and you haven't mentioned the need for medicine."

The wind died out of my sails, and I sank back into the leather upholstery of the booth. I was tired. Too tired to argue about drink choices. Root beer actually was one of my favorite treats, but he didn't know that.

"Can I ask you a question?"

"You can ask." He nodded. I noticed he didn't promise to answer.

"Have you always done this, or did you do something else before?"

"Before what?" His lips quirked up.

"Before whatever this is." I gestured between us.

"What is it you think you know?"

I sighed. I should have known better than to think I'd get a straight answer out of him.

"Well, I don't think you had any real grievance against that guy back home. I think you were there because you were told to be there. And you didn't kill me right away because you were waiting to hear from your boss. Is that right?" I kept my voice low, even though there were only two other booths with customers—and they were on the other end of the diner, I didn't want to draw attention to us. And I got a feeling, he wouldn't appreciate any unwanted attention, either.

He studied me silently with the same intensity I'd found in him the night at the bar. He'd been reserved, but his dominating presence had been palpable. Maybe that's what drew me to him. I figured he'd shoot me down straightaway, and I could crawl home with my failure.

"I spent three tours overseas. Navy SEAL," he said. He didn't move his gaze from me, but I noticed his fingers pressed harder into the table.

"A Navy SEAL?" I blew out a breath. I wasn't surprised. Hell, looking at him, how could I be. The man was basically a brick-and-mortar version of every soldier story I ever heard.

"I finished up my last tour and headed out of the military."

"Why?" I couldn't help the question; it just popped out.

"Family issue." He swiped his hand through the air. His attempt at ending the line of questioning. A moment later, my plate with a cheeseburger and an overabundance of fries was placed in front of me.

"Can I get you folks anything else?" the waitress asked after his plate and the drinks were put on the table.

Dustan swung his gaze from me to the waitress. "No thanks. Just some privacy." He gave her a slow wink.

"Not a problem. Just wave if you need me." Light pink dusted her cheeks. She patted my shoulder. "A keeper," she muttered and headed off, leaving me to deal with him on my own.

"Is there anyone you can't control?" I asked when she was gone, and he started to cut into his burger.

He looked up at me with a grin. "Haven't found a situation yet."

I sighed.

"Eat up, darlin'." He pointed his knife at my plate. "Five hours before we get to our stopping point for the night, remember. And once we get there, you're going to need your energy."

"You can't seriously think I'm going to let you—well, you know." I picked up a fry.

"Isn't an issue of your willingness." He took a large bite of his burger. A drop of ketchup lingered on his lip, but he swiped it away with a napkin.

I turned the topic away from my impending doom and back to him.

"What was the family issue that brought you home?" I picked up my burger, inspecting it for the best place to take my first bite.

His features tightened. "My sister died."

I swallowed my bite, wishing my question could go down with it.

"Oh. I'm so sorry," I whispered. If anyone knew the pain of family loss, it was me.

"Killed herself." He bit into his burger, as though to keep from saying anything more.

"Oh my god," I gasped. "That's—I'm—"

"It's fucked up. But it's over. She had a shit time, and I wasn't home to protect her from it." He took a long pull of his root beer.

"You can't blame—"

"I don't." He cut me off.

I recalled the feverish actions after I made a stupid comment about my worth. Those words had struck him. I hadn't really meant them, not the way he heard them, but the pain I triggered was real to him.

"So, now you work outside the law?" I asked after a few more bites of my burger.

"Outside the law?" He chuckled. "Yeah. Something like that."

"Your boss didn't want me dead—which I'm extremely grateful for, by the way, but if he had. You would have..." I let the question die. "Never mind."

His tongue ran along the inside of his cheek, and he tossed his napkin on top of his mostly eaten food. "If he makes you a target..." His answer faded away. "Then I'll make a decision."

"That's not exactly reassuring," I said, pushing my plate away from me. I'd eaten most of my burger and nearly all of the fries. Another bite and his answer would trigger my reflex to lose all of it on the table.

He waved for the waitress, who seemed to understand he wanted the check. Silently, she dropped it and left us again. Maybe the severity of his expression scared her as much as it had me, the first time I'd seen it.

Dustan pulled out his wallet and dropped several bills on top of the check while scooting out of the booth. He held his hand out to help me out but didn't let me go once I was on my feet.

He led me to the bathroom. It was going to be a long ride until we stopped, so I didn't argue. When I came back out, he cupped my elbow and walked me out to the car.

He opened my door but stopped me from climbing inside. I looked up at him, sure I'd see more of the same fire and irritation glaring down at me. I'd pushed and asked a question he couldn't give me a good answer to.

"I've worked for the Cavalieri De Morte for ten years. The men I work with are my brothers, and the man I take orders from has my complete loyalty. I have never, not once second guessed his orders, and I've never considered if I would follow them or not."

The wind blew between us, whipping my hair around my face. He captured a strand and tucked it behind my ear.

"Until now."

"Okay," I said touching my fingertips to his arm.

"Okay." He nodded, like he'd made a decision. "Get in." He let me go and gestured toward the car. "Five hours until your ass is mine."

And with that firmly spoken promise, he shut the door on any protest I could conjure.

DUSTAN

I have no explanation why I told Cherise about Ellen. I haven't mentioned my sister's suicide since it happened. To anyone.

I lied when I said I didn't blame myself. Because I did. Every fucking day I woke up and remembered that my little sister had been in so much fucking pain and I hadn't seen it, hadn't been there for her, I blamed myself. I never should have left her with our parents.

Joining the SEALs, that was my escape, and eventually Ellen had made hers.

Cherise didn't remind me of Ellen at all. Where my sister was soft and sweet, Cherise was snarky and fierce. They were complete opposites, except when it came to family. Neither of them seemed to have family that had their back.

Ellen had had me, but I was thousands of miles away and silent for weeks at a time. Even if she told me how much she was hurting, how scared she was of living, I was too far away to help. The people who should have been protecting her, watching over her, they let her down.

Like Cherise.

The hotel was just up ahead on the road, and Cherise was dead asleep beside me in the car. She hadn't spoken much since the dinner, and I didn't stir up any conversations, either. The silence gave me a place to hide away and force the memories of my sister out of my head.

After parking my car at the back entrance of the hotel, I looked through my wallet to find my key. Check-ins didn't exactly give me the cover I needed when I traveled. Having my own room to use whenever needed worked with my lifestyle.

I checked my phone for messages then sent a quick text off to Bobby, asking him for an update. He never took so long to get information for me, and I was beginning to wonder how deep Cherise's family ties went with families like the Merdes.

"Are we here?" She stretched her arms over her head and yawned. I smiled at the cuteness before me but straightened up when she peered at me.

"Yeah. We're here." I popped open my door and climbed. After grabbing my bags from the trunk and getting her out of her seat, I led her through the back entrance and up the stairs to my room at the top.

Her brow wrinkled when I produced my master key from my wallet, but she kept her question to herself. For the first time since we'd left my house earlier.

Cherise walked to the bed and sat on the corner, wrapping her arms around her stomach. Her hair poofed up in the back from her nap in the car, giving her a soft look, reminding me she wasn't a criminal. She was an innocent caught up in a fucked-up mangled mess.

I dropped the bags and locked the door.

"There's only one bed." She hooked her ankle over the other.

"Yeah." I nodded. "There was only one in my room last night, too."

She turned away, checking out the rest of the room. "I think I'll shower," she said.

"Might want to rethink that, darlin'," I said, unbuckling my belt. For the last hour of the drive, I'd been envisioning her creamy ass bent over the bed, waiting for her much-deserved punishment. I would have lingered more on the vision of my belt leaving red stripes across the generously round cheeks, but I didn't need my fucking cock to start bursting in my pants.

"Why?" She stopped just outside the bathroom and looked my way. Her gaze dropped to my hands, at the leather being pulled free from my slacks, and her complexion paled.

"From what I've heard, a belting on a wet ass is worse. But if you want to make it worse on yourself, I suppose I can wait." I folded my belt over, making sure the buckle was tucked securely in my palm.

"Dustan. It's not my fault that asshole came onto your property." She fisted her hands at her sides, showing me her fire while fear lingered in her eyes.

"No, but it is your fault you were walking the exact place I told you not to walk, isn't it?" I asked, not taking a step or losing an inch of ground.

Her throat worked as she stared at my belt dangling at my side. She didn't want to admit wanting it, but she wanted this part of me. She responded to my dominant side.

"I don't want…"

"Come over here, darlin'." I raised my hand, beckoning her to me.

Indecision warred in her gaze when it met mine.

"I can't let you—"

"You aren't letting me. You're being a good girl and taking your punishment. If you don't, and you start acting like a bad girl, what happens?"

She licked her lips. "Bad things happen to bad girls."

"That's right. And good things happen to good girls, remember that, darlin'." My cock stirred in my pants. Just remembering the heat of her pussy clenching around my fingers when I brought her to orgasm after her whipping, made me ready to take her—hard.

She took the five steps between us and stood at the foot of the bed.

"Strip down," I ordered and tossed the belt onto the bed so I could shake off my jacket.

With jerky movements, she tugged the sweater and jeans off, but by the time she'd gotten to her underwear, she'd slowed down. Her breathing picked up, making her breasts rise and fall with the quickened pace.

I kept my focus on her eyes while I unbuttoned my shirt and peeled it from my body. Her bottom lip slipped between her teeth as I exposed my torso. Ink covered my chest and my abs, most of my shoulders were tatted as well. Forty-seven tattoos in all, that's what I had on my body. Some phrases that resonated with me, others images I liked. Fifteen names littered my chest, each one a man I knew. Men I'd fought side by side with and protected as best I could until it wasn't enough. Fallen brothers in battle, never to be forgotten.

"Hand me the belt, darlin'." I held my hand out, waiting for her to comply.

"You don't have to do this." A tremor ran through her voice, but she turned around and picked up the belt anyway. She had to know I wouldn't change my mind. I never did.

I took the leather strap from her and let my gaze wander over her curves. Sinking my teeth into those hips became a high priority the longer I stared at her.

Stepping closer to her, I grasped her chin between my thumb and finger. I pushed her head back until she was eye to eye with me. "I think if I don't, you'll wish I had."

A soft pink hue covered her cheeks, and I grinned.

"That's not true," she whispered. The struggle played out in her eyes. She wanted to be strong, firm in her denial, but I could see the truth. It was right there in front of me. The blush, the dilated pupils, the way her tongue ran along her lips.

"Oh, I think it is. I think if I touched your pussy right now, I'd find it soaking wet for me. And I know when we're done here, you'll be a mess for me." The more I spoke, the redder her cheeks became, and every ounce of me fucking loved it.

"It's just a response. Not real." She tried to tug away from my grip, but I intensified it.

Her nipples brushed against my chest when I leaned closer to her. I inhaled, deep and long, enjoying the scent of her fear mixed with arousal. I couldn't quite tell if it was the belting or the arousal she feared more. It didn't really matter in the end. I wanted both from her, and Cherise was turning out to be a very giving person.

"We'll see. Now, turn around and press your chest

to the bed. Your ass is to stay high up for me. If I have to stop to correct your position, it will be worse."

"Worse than the tree?" her question popped out, surprising her almost as much as me, I thought.

I blinked. "Let's hope we don't have to relive the tree anytime soon." I'd been hard on her, as hard as I had ever been on anyone. This time she hadn't earned that severity, but she had earned a solid tanning.

Her throat worked as she swallowed, probably another of her smart-ass remarks. She couldn't seem to stop them when she got nervous.

"Okay. Okay," she said, but I suspected she was talking herself into accepting the situation more than she was letting me know she was ready.

I released her chin and gestured for her to get in position. Since she wasn't overly tall, the top of her head barely level with my collarbone, she managed the position easily. She folded her hands beneath her cheek and turned away.

Not one to waste time, I unleashed the belt across her ass. Her yelp of surprise filled the room just after the sharp snap of the leather. Her cheeks jiggled with the force, but I didn't let myself focus too long on the erotic dance of her flesh.

"Fuck!" she screamed out and started to rise.

"Stay." I snapped the belt across her thighs, and she cried out again, still trying to get up. "What did I say about position?" I said, irritated she still hadn't learned I meant what I said.

"I can't! It fucking hurts, Dustan!"

I shoved between her shoulder blades until her face was back in the mattress. Pressing my knee into her back, I held her down and brought the belt across her ass and thighs over and over again, not giving her a moment of peace or space enough to take a deep breath. She wiggled and cried, but she wasn't going anywhere with my weight pressed against her.

Ugly red marks crisscrossed her ass and the tops of her thighs. The bruises from the last whipping hadn't healed, but I made sure to avoid the welts. Her ass damn glowed nearly red by the time I was finished with her, and she was sobbing beneath me. Somewhere between my knee hitting her back and my stopping, she'd given up the fight. Her body trembled with her sobs.

I tossed the belt to the floor and sat beside her on the bed. Pulling her up in my arms, I dragged her into my lap. She pressed her head into the crook of my neck and hugged me tight.

She hugged me.

I'd just unleashed a hell of a spanking on her, and she was snuggling into me, not running away.

I smoothed her hair away from her face, wiping the wet tracks from her tears as well. I cupped her ass, feeling the heat but also checking if I'd given her any more welts.

I hadn't.

I'd been careful. My aim wasn't to damage her. Realizing that, my hands stilled. I froze.

I didn't want her harmed.

I'd punished her for putting herself in harm's way.

Any time, Arthur could put a target on her head, and I was worried about her well-being. This wasn't my job.

I wasn't supposed to be caring for her. I was supposed to be holding onto her until Arthur figured out what to do with her.

"I'm sorry I tried to get up." Her whispered apology shot heat through my veins.

I fisted my hand in her hair, pulled her back from my body, and looked own at her. Her puffy eyes and red nose should have made her look a complete wreck.

The mess should have revolted me, but instead, my cock stiffened in my pants.

"I'm not," I confessed and captured her mouth below mine.

CHERISE

The burn in my ass couldn't compare to the heat running between my legs. He'd been right. I was wet before I even bent over for him. But now, with my ass on fire, my tears drying on my cheeks, my pussy ached for his touch.

When his lips touched mine, the tension in my body melted away. I touched his cheek, feeling the rough stubble of a beard. He pressed his body against me, moving me down to my back.

I hissed when the blanket rubbed against my ass, and he pulled back, looking down at me.

"Your ass is going to be a mess if you keep being bad for me," he said with a lazy grin. He probably wouldn't mind seeing his belt markings across my ass every day.

He leaned down, pressing kisses to my cheeks and down my neck until he reached my breasts. His fingers dug into my hips as he lashed my nipple with his tongue. I arched my back, offering myself to him, needing him to put out the fire he'd started.

"How wet are you, darlin'?" he asked, moving a hand between my legs. I spread my thighs for him, craving his touch as much as I needed the next beat of my heart.

"Very," I answered while staring up into his eyes. He seemed to like watching me, to see how I'd react to his words—his touch.

His fingers found my clit as though he'd memorized the road map of my body. I sucked in a hot breath with his touch. He rubbed the bundle of nerves in a circle, pressing down hard, all the while watching me. His gaze igniting me from the inside.

I grabbed his shoulders. He'd only just touched me, and I was ready to explode.

"Nah, uh, darlin'. Not yet." He grinned down at me, exposing a little crease on the side of his mouth when he did. I wanted to bite that cheek.

"Please," I pleaded, wiggling beneath his touch.

"Not yet." He slid off the bed, away from me. I groaned, not even caring how telling the sound probably was. I looked down the length of my body at him as he unbuttoned his slacks and pushed them over his hips, along with what looked like boxers. I didn't focus on the underwear type for too long, not after his cock sprang free.

I swallowed hard. The urge to reach out and feel him, to wrap my fingers around his thick shaft and sense his warmth consumed me. But I was learning Dustan's ways quickly. If he didn't tell me to do it, I wasn't going to risk his displeasure by acting without permission.

He climbed back on the bed, moving me over to the middle.

"Part these beautiful legs for me." He tapped my thighs.

I stared at him in silence for a beat then slid my legs apart.

He captured my face between his hands and kissed me again. Deeper and with more force than before, knocking all sense and reason from my mind as the tip of his cock touched my entrance. I ran my hand around his neck and up into his hair.

Heat ran through my body, speeding through my veins and making everything tingle.

"Cherise." My name escaped his lips in a raspy, dark sound between kisses. "Open up for me, darlin'."

His cock drove in, the large tip pushing into me,

but then he stopped.

Dark eyes leered down at me. His fingers gripped my cheeks harder, making me wince.

"Tell me no," he commanded. "Tell me no, and I'll stop right now."

Stop? Nothing could hurt more than him stopping at that moment.

I touched his cheek.

"I'm not saying no," I whispered, feeling in my heart he needed to hear that.

"If you don't say no, I'm taking you, darlin'. And when I take something, I don't let go." His forehead wrinkled, and his words hit hard.

"I'm not saying no," I repeated.

He stared down at me for a long moment before seeming to come to a decision.

"Good." He let go of my cheeks and crushed my lips with his own. He slammed into me, his cock filling me, stretching me. I cried out from the sudden intrusion, the overfilling sensation, but he continued to kiss me, taking my cries and my pleasure into his own body.

He pulled back and rocked into me again, and again. I raised my legs, hooking my ankles over his ass as he continued to fuck me without restraint.

"Fuck," he muttered, pulling halfway out again.

"Dustan." I dug my fingertips into his shoulder. "Don't stop."

He looked down at me, his breath ragged, several locks of dark hair hanging loose over his forehead.

"Never." He plowed forward. "I can't be soft with you," he said between thrusts.

"Don't. I don't…fuck…I don't want…fuck!" My body wound up, ready to spring into oblivion as he ground his hips into me with each new thrust of his cock. "Not gentle," I said, hoping I finished my thought in a way he'd understand. I didn't want his softness. I wanted this. The raw, animalistic claiming.

"Oh, fuck, fuck, fuck, fuck," I chanted, feeling the tension peak. My eyes widened as my body sprang free of the buildup, and I screamed. I yelled his name and any other word that popped into my head while my body catapulted through the electricity he'd ignited.

"That's it, darlin'. That's it," he cheered as I slowly sailed back to him. He pressed a soft kiss to the tip of my nose and wiped the hair from my face. "Gorgeous," he whispered and began thrusting into me again. Slow but firm strokes dragged me back to him, and I gripped his shoulders, sinking my fingernails deep.

He growled, a low and sultry sound that should have warned me the animal was being unleashed. But I was too caught up in the fire burning in his eyes, in the raw beauty of him as he took me harder and harder still to heed any caution. I arched my back, taking him even deeper. He stretched me, fucked me, hurt me, and every thrust of his hips brought another round of painful pleasure.

"Fuck!" he ground out between clenched teeth. He hooked his arm beneath my knee, yanking my leg up, and intensified his movements. His jaw tensed as his hips rocked harder and faster. I sensed his need matched my own. Felt him teetering on the edge that would throw him into the abyss with me.

Another sharp thrust, and he stilled, his body firm while his release whisked him away.

He rested his forehead against mine, collecting his breath but still stealing mine. I ran my hand down his back, feeling for the first time raised scars. How had he been hurt? And by whom?

"Dustan." I wanted to ask him, but when he leaned up and looked into my eyes, the question died away. The darkness seemed to ebb away, and now he was just—him. No anger or danger, just a man staring down at me with concern and longing.

"Did I hurt you?" he asked.

I laughed. "You like when you hurt me," I pointed out.

"Usually," he agreed with a smile. "But I didn't go easy."

I brushed his hair from his forehead. "I didn't want easy."

He stared down at me for a long time before slipping free. His hot seed ran out of me, but I didn't move. I watched him as he climbed out of the bed and disappeared into the bathroom. When he returned, he had a towel in his hand.

"Open your legs," he ordered, and I obeyed, letting him clean me. He ran the warm, wet cloth through my folds, between my ass cheeks and over my thighs.

Once he was finished, he took the towel back into

the bathroom. I slid off the bed, grabbing my sweater and shoved it back on. Catching a glimpse of myself in the mirror, I turned my ass toward it to see the damage.

"Shit." I touched a red stripe.

"Tomorrow's car ride is going to be rough for you, so I wouldn't go being bad again for a while," he said from behind me.

I saw him in the mirror, sliding his boxers up over his hips. It wasn't enough to hide the deliciousness of his body, but I forced my gaze back to my ass.

The warmth rushing through my chest when I pressed down on the marks surprised me. Shouldn't I be repelled by the lashings? Instead, I was almost proud of them, and I definitely enjoyed seeing them.

I yanked my sweater down and stomped over to the bed. Space between us would clear my head. He was twisting me into some sort of sick woman who got off on his arrogance and authority. He was fucking with my head.

I pulled the covers down and climbed into bed. I faced away from him and tucked the blanket beneath my chin. Somewhere along the way, I'd forgotten my goal was to get the hell away from him, not be claimed by him, not belong to him in any way.

The bed dipped behind me as he got beneath the covers with me. He flicked off the lights over the bed and tossed his arm over my waist, dragging me toward him. I bit down on my tongue when my ass hit him.

"Whatever you're doing to yourself in that head of yours, you should stop. Getting lost up there won't help," he said with the same level tone he always used.

"I'm tired. That's all," I lied.

He squeezed my middle. "Try again, darlin'."

"You don't get to know every thought that crosses my mind." I punched the pillow beneath my head and wiggled beneath his arm—but he wouldn't let me go.

He released a deep breath. "Get some sleep. It's a long drive tomorrow."

"Are you finally going to tell me where the hell we're going?" I asked, letting my frustration show.

He pinched my hip. "Watch that attitude, darlin'. Ask me real nice, and maybe I'll answer."

I bit my lip, determined not to give in to him. Which lasted all of a minute.

"Dustan, can you please tell me where we're going?"

He kissed my shoulder. "New Orleans."

I tensed. "Why?"

"Because that's where Arthur is, and that's who we are going to see." He hugged me tighter to him. "No more questions. Get some sleep."

Sleep? Who the hell could sleep after that?

DUSTAN

Cherise slept like the dead. It had taken me two slaps to her ass and the threat of a full-on spanking to get her out of bed, but she finally complied. I chose to ignore the nasty glare she shot at me while she scooted to the bathroom with her clothes to shower and dress. I even gave her space when we climbed into my car to start the drive.

After an hour on the road, I'd pulled off the highway and driven through to get her a breakfast sandwich. She hadn't said anything, but her stomach had been growling for twenty minutes. Whatever she was thinking, she was really getting herself twisted into some serious knots.

When I handed her the sandwich, she'd taken and unwrapped it without a word, and I'd still let her have her space.

But we were five hours in and would be at Arthur's estate in another two. She needed to get whatever her problem was solved by then. I didn't need to worry about her shooting her mouth off to Arthur while we were there. I just needed his final decision and information so I could make my next move with her. If she got on his bad side, started pissing him off, she could make everything go sideways for both of us.

"Ready to tell me what's eating you?" I asked, turning off the radio.

She glanced over at me then refocused her attention on the road in front of us.

"I shouldn't have let you—I mean I shouldn't have." She stopped talking and growled. A cute, rough sound that probably didn't truly emulate the powerful regret she was holding close to her chest. "Last night was a mistake," she finally blurted.

"Which part?" I asked.

"What?"

"Which part was a mistake? When I spanked you, or when I fucked you?"

I could practically feel her cheeks heating up from the driver's seat.

"Or was it that you liked both that's the mistake? Or that you needed both?" I would pull the truth from her, even if I had to stop the car.

She exhaled like it took all her energy to do so. I reached across the center console and grabbed her hand, lacing our fingers together.

"You've never had a man smack your ass before?" I forced a lightness to my question. She was already spooked enough because of her reactions the night before.

"No." She shook her head and kept her eyes focused on our entangled hands.

"I'm not going to let anything happen to you," I said, squeezing her hand.

"I shouldn't have—" She exhaled again and pushed her head back against the headrest of her seat.

"You shouldn't have enjoyed it. You should have hated every second of my touch." I supplied the words for her worry when she seemed unable to get them out on her own.

"You're not a good man," she whispered.

I squeezed her hand again. "I'm not. That's right."

"You'll hurt me if I don't do what you say."

"I'll punish you, yes," I agreed.

"And if Arthur tells you to get rid of me...you will." And there it was.

The real worry.

The real question. Would I go against Arthur if

he put a target on her head?

When no one else could understand me, Arthur did. When I had nothing but my skills and my anger to keep me alive, Arthur put them to good use. We weren't good men, but we were good to each other.

"We aren't at that bridge yet, darlin'. Don't try crossing it just yet." I ran my thumb over her palm. It was the only comfort I could give her.

"The bridge you're going to throw me off of?" She tried to laugh but ended up sucking in a breath and closing her eyes. The tension in her hand grew and, for the first time in as long as I could remember, I wanted to promise everything would be all right.

"We have another hour before we get there," I said and let her hand go, patting her knee. "Don't get yourself all worked up. I told you—when I take something, I don't let go."

She turned the radio on, filling the car with music

to block out the conversation we couldn't have.

We finished the drive without any more conversation. I would let her have some peace, but I wouldn't let her crawl back into her head though. When she started to pull away, I reached over and held her hand. When she went too still, I pinched her thigh. I kept her with me in the present. Because diving into the future was too uncertain, and slipping into the past was too dangerous.

CHERISE

My stomach twisted into a tangled knot when Dustan parked outside Arthur's mansion. Not exactly what I expected from an underworld boss, but I supposed that's what he wanted. The lawns and gardens were perfectly manicured and beautiful. The entire estate was meticulously groomed. Somehow the perfection made me more nervous. If Arthur found me lacking, would he have Dustan kill me right there?

I flipped down the visor and checked myself in the mirror. I didn't have any makeup or my flat iron. The motel shampoo hadn't been very generous, and the conditioner had been a joke. My hair was dull and all over the place. Random curls poked out everywhere, and the fragranced soap had left my cheeks red.

Dustan laughed softly from the driver's side where his keys dangled from his fingers. "You look fine, darlin'."

I sighed.

"You don't lie very well," I said with an eye roll.

He grabbed my chin and twisted my head to make me look at him. "I have never and will never lie to you, Cherise. When I say you look fine, you do."

I studied his face, the severity of his frown, the darkness edging its way back into his eyes. He took these moments of self-depreciation seriously.

"Okay." I touched his wrist.

"You're still nervous." He didn't let my chin go.

"Wouldn't you be?" I asked quietly.

"He won't hurt you."

"That's what he has you for."

"Arthur isn't unreasonable. I will find a way to

make this okay. For everyone." The loyalty Dustan felt toward Arthur rang through his statement, but his vow to keep me safe lingered there between the words.

I nodded because what else could I do? Dustan, as scary, as dangerous, as strict as he was, had not lied to me since we met. He'd whipped me, spanked me, fucked me, kidnapped me, but he had never been dishonest. An odd trait for a killer—honesty—but there it was. And if he said he'd make this okay, I had to believe him. "Okay."

"You're not even going to talk to him, okay? You're safe here, but I don't want you wandering around. Once I get us settled in our room, you are going to stay there—right?" He brushed a hair from my face with the tips of his fingers. Just the light dusting of his touch sent a shiver through me, waking my desire for more.

"Of course," I promised, the tenderness in my ass

reminding me of what crossing him would result.

He scrutinized me with suspicious eyes before breaking into a chuckle and letting my chin go. "I'm not sure your ass could handle another spanking, darlin'. Be good for me today." He trailed a fingertip along my jaw. "Really good things come to good girls."

I swallowed, trying to get rid of the dry scratch in my throat. When he looked at me like that, like a deep-rooted hunger was taking him over, all my nerve endings fired up, waiting for him to calm them again.

"Okay," I said.

He brushed his lips across mine then pressed his lips to my ear. "When I have you alone tonight in my bed, I'm going to lick every inch of you. And when I have you squirming and crying for me, begging me to let you come—I'm going to fuck you so hard you'll scream for me. I love when you scream for me, darlin'. Your cries are too beautiful to keep from me."

Tingles shot straight to my pussy. I went wet, saturating my panties and craving his cock. Fuck, I wanted him to do all of those things and more.

He bit my earlobe then pulled back, touching his finger to my lips when I started to speak.

"Be a good girl so I can deliver on my promise." He tapped my mouth.

I barely registered his words before his door was open and then mine flew open as well. He was there, helping me out. How'd he get around the car so fast?

His damn promises had me all muddled. He'd probably planned it that way, to keep me quiet, to keep me obedient as he led me up the steps to the entrance of the gorgeous New Orleans mansion.

The inside of the mansion warranted a longer look than Dustan allowed. The decor, the furniture, the ambiance all gave the very distinct impression of wealth, but more than money—a wealth of power.

Dustan didn't give me time to take it all in before whisking me up a set of winding stairs to the second floor. He tugged on my hand when I slowed to admire a painting, and cast a stern glare over his shoulder when I tried to dig in.

"I just wanted to see something," I muttered as he swung me toward a door and produced a key from his pocket.

"Not now. Maybe later," he said as he slid the key into the lock. I wouldn't get to wander. He'd already made that clear to me in the car, which meant he'd have to take me on a tour. And with the fierceness of his set jaw as an indicator, I settled myself that I wouldn't get that tour.

"If being here makes you tense, why are we here?" I asked once in the room. "Shit." I gasped when he flipped on the lights and the suite illuminated before me. It wasn't a bedroom but a living area with dark-brown leather couches and dark-stained wood tables to accentuate the sensuality of the room. It didn't have a gaudy feeling to it, rather it had warmth.

"There's a bathroom through there." Dustan, obviously not as breath-taken by the room as me, walked through the room and pointed to a closed door. "The bedroom's here, another bathroom is attached with a shower and tub." He slid the double doors along their tracks to reveal the bedroom.

"What, no kitchen?" I tried to joke, but I was still taking in the room. I'd never seen such luxury before. The wood flooring had to have cost more than my rent for an entire year. Alternating between three dark hues, it lightened the severity of the room.

"There's snacks and drinks if you want." He showed me the wood-paneled mini fridge. It blended in with the rest of the furniture, making it look more like a cabinet.

My gaze roamed over to him. "Snacks."

His brow wrinkled. "Yeah. Everything you need is in here, so no excuse to leave this suite."

"Are there other men like you living here?" I asked. He'd led me down a long hallway of doors to his room.

"We all have our own suites. No one is expecting me except for Arthur, so there shouldn't be any visitors. But if someone knocks, you don't answer, and you don't unlock the door." He jerked his finger toward me.

"You don't trust these men you work with?" I tilted my head to the side.

He straightened his stance. "I trust every one of them with my life. And yours. But until I have this all situated, you stay in here."

"You've been tense since we got here. Why?" I moved toward him. "Should I be worried? Should

I maybe hide in case you come back with your gun drawn again?" My nervousness ramped up my facade. He could very well return to execute me. He'd made no promises to go against Arthur if I was too much of a loose end to deal with.

He met me in the middle of the room, capturing my shoulders with his hands and running them up and down my arms. "I'll worry about that. You just be a good girl for me and stay in here."

"You think calling me a good girl will just send me into some sort of obedient trance," I accused in a soft voice. He wasn't exactly wrong, but I wanted him to be. I wanted those words to have a hell of a lot less effect on me than they did.

"Do you remember what I said would be your reward if you don't get into any trouble?" His thumbs caressed my skin, sending little jolts of electricity through me.

"Yes." I nodded, trying to play it off. Like all the promises of ecstasy hadn't made my insides gooey.

"Just remind yourself of that if you start getting an itch to be a bad girl." He gave my arms a squeeze then released me. "Because what happens to bad girls, Cherise?"

He opened the door and waited there, the glow of the hallway surrounding him and casting him in shadow.

"Bad things happen to bad girls." I repeated his words to him.

His gaze wandered over me. "That's right. And a lot of bad things can happen here. There's rooms built for just that sort of thing." And with that, he stepped into the hall and closed the door. The bolt slid into place.

DUSTAN

"Dustan." Arthur greeted me when I stepped into his office. I closed the door behind me and made my way to his desk to shake his hand.

"It's been a while," I said, releasing his hand and taking my seat across the desk from him.

"You don't come down here often," he remarked.

"Chicago's home." I grinned. My childhood home, now run-down from years of neglect, resided on the south side of the city. Even after everything that happened, I couldn't leave Chicago.

"Hmmm." He nodded. "And Cherise Styles, she's with you?" Direct and to the point. Arthur was all business. I never had to guess what he was thinking or where I stood with him. He laid it out plain.

"Upstairs." I steepled my fingers and crossed my ankle over my knee.

"I have information for you." Arthur dragged a folder from the corner of his desk toward him. "You're not going to like it."

The muscles in my neck tensed. If I wasn't going to like it—I'd fucking hate it.

"Okay, what is it?" I asked.

"Your intel guy, that friend of yours."

"Bobby, yeah?" I leaned forward.

Arthur picked up the folder but didn't hand it to me.

"He's changed teams." He dropped the folder on my side of the desk, but I didn't reach for it. Arthur had more to say and, until he finished, I wasn't touching it.

"What makes you say that?"

"That folder has everything you need to know

about Cherise Styles and her family. It took one phone call to get my hands on it. She wasn't hard to track down, her family not hidden or protected. Bobby's been jerking you around because he's trying to make a deal behind your back with the Merde family."

My teeth clenched while my heart sank lower in my chest. Hot rage dragged through me. "You're sure?"

Arthur tilted his head. Of course, he was sure. He wouldn't be telling me if he didn't have every confidence in the information he handed over. He wouldn't give his men bad intel.

I picked up the folder and opened it. Bobby had been taking money from the Merde family. He'd given up my safe house. My fingers tensed around the edges of the folder, crumbling them.

"That farm up in Minnesota doesn't belong to her uncle, it's your girl's. One hundred percent hers. Rolled over to her when her parents were killed." He wasn't giving me new information, but I sensed more was coming.

"The house fire?" I asked, already sensing the dread building in my stomach.

"Yes, but it was arson. That fire was meant to take out the whole family. Cherise was supposed to be home that weekend from college," Arthur went on. "Her uncle has a large-scale farm, growing poppies."

"She's under the impression the farm grows poppy seeds? I'm guessing it doesn't," I asked, a little rattled by the information being spilled to me. Bobby had known all of this. He'd had all of this at his fingertips and withheld it from me.

"The Styles farm is the largest Midwest grower for the Merde family. From what I could find out, her father didn't want to expand into the second section of the farm. He wanted out altogether, but his brother saw the potential.

"Merde gave permission for the family to be taken out. When Cherise survived, she was sent back to finish college—not welcomed back home. Randall Styles, her uncle, made it clear she wasn't to come home. He convinced the Merdes she wouldn't be a problem. But then they saw her on that tape at the bar."

"Antonio." I nodded. The night we met. The night all of this began.

"They want her taken out?"

Arthur shook his head. "No, but her uncle does."

"He wants the farm legally. Why not just have her sign it over to him? She already thinks she did."

"She signed over her inheritance, yes." He tapped his temple. "Not a smart one to do that."

"She was overwhelmed," I defended her. She'd lost her parents and her uncle—who she feared for a reason I was going to figure out—forced her out of her family home. I knew what that pain was—to lose the love of family and see no hope for the future.

Arthur examined me silently for a beat. "I'm sure that's what it was. Her uncle used her grief to his benefit. But the land has been in a trust, and now it's fully hers."

"And he wants her dead because he thinks he can't get her to sign it over?"

Arthur lifted a shoulder. "I assume. Does it matter? He wants her gone."

I sank back into my chair.

"She's an innocent," I said softly.

Arthur remained silent.

"The Merde family is helping her uncle get rid of her so he can keep growing for them? Not even trying to get her to cooperate?" I worked out the scenario in my head.

"Sometimes making the problem go away is easier." Arthur rested his fingertips on the edge of his desk.

"You have a directive on this?" I asked with a raised chin. "Taking out Antonio for them started all this."

"True," Arthur agreed. "This is fallout from your assignment." He stood from his desk. "How you handle it is up to you, but I would suggest getting her to let go of that farm. The Merde family won't like losing their biggest grower in the Midwest."

"I'll handle it." I got to my feet.

"And Bobby?" Arthur's eyebrow arched.

"He gave up my safe house to the Merdes. He'll pay for that."

"I know he's a friend—"

"Betrayal isn't something to be forgiven," I said with finality.

Arthur gave a curt nod. "You'll handle it the way you know how. Anything you need, just ask."

"Of course." I opened his office door to find a beautiful woman headed toward us. I flashed a grin over my shoulder at Arthur. "I'll leave you to your business. We'll be spending the night but will be gone by breakfast."

Arthur gestured for the woman to make her way inside. "Safe travels," he said, but his eyes were already focused on his next meeting. I left him to it, and quietly shut the door behind me.

I pulled out my phone and checked for messages from Bobby. Still nothing, but I didn't expect anything. The botched attempt on my estate would make him run scared. He'd suspect I was on to him.

I climbed the stairs toward my suite. Usually while in New Orleans, I'd enjoy myself in the club. Maybe grab a girl for some fun for the evening. But this wasn't a typical visit. And I already had someone waiting for me in my bed. Someone I had promised to make squeal with pleasure.

Bobby's betrayal sucked the breath out of my lungs, but Cherise—she'd be able to put it back.

I'd finally figured out the television settings and snuggled beneath a blanket on the couch when the door to Dustan's suite opened. He stormed in and slammed it, rattling the frame. A dark storm raged in his eyes, sending a lightning bolt through my body when his glare landed on me.

I pulled the soft cashmere blanket up to my chin and sank back into the cushions. His fingers stretched out at his sides. My mouth dried. I'd seen that look before, and he'd been holding a gun at the time. He was ready to kill.

"I stayed in the room," I said weakly. It hadn't even occurred to me to go wandering around. The sort of men there weren't exactly in my typical circle.

He shook his head like he was trying to shake away his anger, but I could see it bubbling, ready to explode.

Had Arthur given him orders to take care of me? I bit down on the inside of my cheek, unsure if I should speak or move. It seemed anything could set him off at that moment. My heart ping-ponged its way through my chest, making thinking impossible.

Without a word, he shook out of his suit jacket and tossed it on a chair. With his eyes glued to me, he unbuttoned his sleeves and began to undo the row of buttons on his shirt, ripping it from his body once he was done. The shirt landed on the floor.

I swallowed, blinking back tears. There wasn't anywhere for me to run. Every inch outside of that room was as dangerous if not more than the space inside it. He'd said there were rooms for bad things.

The blanket trapped the heat of my body, making me shiver in a cold sweat as I watched him start toward me. His white deco tee stretched across his broad chest, making it easy to see his muscles rippling as he moved. He stopped when he got to the arm of the couch. Three cushions. Only three cushions separated us, and with one step he'd be right on me.

My fingers loosened on the blanket, letting it fall into my lap.

"What happened?" I asked, still leery about knowing. If Arthur had called for my demise, would Dustan tell me?

"Good and bad," he said in clipped words. "Mostly bad."

I swallowed and pressed a hand to my stomach. The swirling emotions kicked up into hurricane strength when he didn't continue talking.

"Bad for me."

He wiped his hand over his face, scratching at the stubble growing on his jaw. "No, darlin'. You're safe. Like I said." His tone remained low, dangerous, but his words and the little kick up of his lips softened the air between us.

I shoved the blanket off and crawled across the cushions to the other side of the couch. Getting up on my knees, I rested my hands on his shoulders.

"You're pissed though." I ran my hands over his arms, feeling the tension in his muscles.

"Not at you." He slid both hands around my neck, fisted my hair, and pulled my head back. "You were good for me. You stayed."

I winced at the sting his fingers caused.

"The television sucks," I said, his dark mood stoked my smart-ass side.

His lips spread wide into a grin. "The television is fine, darlin'. The remote's a little confusing."

Were we really talking about the TV? He pulled my head back more, his gaze floating over my face, my neck, my body before returning back to my eyes.

"Take off your clothes." He released me with a little jerk. "I promised you a reward."

I sank back until my ass pressed into my heels and looked him over. He needed a release.

In record time, I removed every stitch of clothing and stood in front of him, waiting. His eyes never left me. He seemed to be soaking me up.

The backs of his fingers skated across my collarbone and down to my breasts. Cupping them, he flicked his thumbs over my nipples. "I love your tits," he said. Some of the darkness crept into his tone, making him sound ragged and raw.

My hands went to his belt, working the leather through the buckle until it hung open at his waist.

"Need something?" He chuckled as I unbuttoned

his slacks and shoved his zipper down.

"You," I said gruffly, slipping my hand into his boxers and wrapping my fingers around his hard shaft. Smooth and warm. I licked my lips.

Without asking, or waiting for direction, I sank down to my knees. Feeling his stress swirling around him, pressing against him. Whatever happened in his meeting, it'd left him rigid with anger. I couldn't fix the big problem, but I could help him now. I could give him the release he needed to relax. Once he was soft again, once he'd expended the angry energy, he'd be able to find his answers.

I let him go and grabbed his slacks, pulling them down to his feet, along with his black cotton boxers. He kicked out of them and fisted his cock in front of my lips, slowly stroking himself until a small bead of pre-cum appeared on the head.

Looking up, I met his gaze and flicked the

moisture from his cock with my tongue and ran it along my upper lip. His jaw tensed, and he grabbed my hair again.

"Hard, darlin', suck hard." He gave me no warning before shoving his dick past my lips and deep into my mouth. I gagged when the tip of his cock hit my throat, but he didn't seem to notice, or he didn't care. He pulled out and slammed back in again. I prepared myself, swallowing him down.

"Fuck, yes." He growled over me and tightened his fist. Tears pricked my eyes, more from the sting in my scalp than his cock filling my throat with every rough stroke.

I remembered his dictate and closed my lips around his thick shaft, sucking hard on him as he continued to fuck my throat. I tried to breathe through my nose, but he cut off my air too easily with his cock. I gasped and pulled back, leaving a mess with all my saliva slipping from my mouth.

He chuckled and leaned down, wiping my chin. "Messy girl." He smeared the spittle over my chest. "I like you messy."

Yanking my head back to look up at him, he ran his thumb across my temple, gathering the tears that had slipped down.

"But I love your tears." He brought his thumb to his lips, suckling on it with a smile.

I wrapped my hand around his cock, enjoying the second his control slipped, and he closed his eyes to the sensation I gave him. I gripped him harder and stroked him, slow at first, mimicking his own actions but then going faster and faster.

"Fuck." He groaned, and his hips thrust toward me. "Your mouth, darlin'. I want your mouth." He tapped my cheek with his hand, soft then hard when I didn't comply right away. "Open for me," he ordered, and dark eyes met mine when I looked up at him.

I parted my lips, and he pushed forward again. I tried to run my tongue along his length, but as in everything with Dustan, he controlled the actions. He fucked my throat again, hard, stretching me and taking away my breath. I steadied myself by pressing my hands to his thighs, his hard, muscular thighs.

As quickly as he'd taken me, he pulled away. "Over the couch," he ordered, retreating a step. I wiped the back of my hand across my mouth and slowly moved to my feet. He ripped off his shirt and tossed it to the floor.

Fuck, he was beautiful. I wanted to touch him, to trace every line of ink, every hard edge of muscle, but he didn't look to be in the patient sort of mood. He grabbed my arm and spun me around, delivering half a dozen slaps to my ass and shoved me over the edge of sanity.

I looked over my shoulder at him. Need. So much fucking need burned in his gaze when he leveled me with his glare. My heart danced beneath him.

"More," I said softly, raising my ass up in the air.

"More what?" he asked with a furrowed brow.

I wiggled my ass, and he laughed.

"More of this?" He slapped me again, and I sighed. "You're already bruised." He leaned over me, his cock pressing against my ass and his lips trailing up my spine. "I can't use my belt, darlin'." He bit down hard on my back and I sucked in air, closing my eyes and letting the burning pain spread to my chest, releasing the tension I'd gathered since he stormed into the room.

He licked the spot he'd marked.

"I need you," he said softly, so quiet that I figured it hadn't been meant for my ears.

I pushed my ass up at him, feeling his cock slip

between my legs, through my folds. "I'm here," I said over my shoulder.

"Exactly where you should be," he ground out and sank his hand into my hair, pulling my head back, stretching my neck as he positioned his dick behind me. I felt the bulbous head of his cock against my entrance, but as much as I wanted to shove my hips at him, I knew he needed this. The control and power. He needed it as much as I did, and I wasn't going to fight him over it.

He slapped my hip, sending a current of sharp pain through my ass just as he plowed forward and filled me with his cock. I cried out at the sudden intrusion, the fullness and stretch his cock created, but he wasn't in a gentle mood.

Thank God.

He took me. He didn't fuck me or make love but seized what was his. Every thrust bucked me harder toward the edge. He grabbed my shoulder, digging his fingernails into my flesh and dragging them down my back. I hissed, curling my spine along with the burn. It fueled him.

His strokes came harder, faster, and all I could make out with any real certainty was the sound of our bodies meeting savagely over and over again. I pressed my hands into the arm of the couch, steadying myself as he continued to pound into me.

"Fuck. Fuck!" I chanted and cried out when his fingers once again scratched along my skin. "Fuck!"

"That's it, darlin'," he said between harsh pants. "That's it."

I stiffened with the next rake of his hand, my mind reeled higher and higher until the fog surrounding me was too thick to see through.

"So close," I cried out. "So close!"

"Let's get you there," he said, but it was from far

away. His hands were on me; he'd let go of my hair and was touching me. My back, my ass, my stomach, everywhere.

I arched my body to give him better access, and he slipped his hand between my pelvis and the couch. Finding my clit without any hesitation, he began to rub hard, matching the rhythm of his cock.

"Fuck! Dustan! Fuck!" I screamed, feeling the peak speeding down at me. The fog cleared, and I spiraled down until the explosion catapulted me up again.

"That's it, come for me, darlin', come." His words followed me, but wave after wave drowned them out.

Slowly, the fog lifted, and I felt him again, felt him moving behind me, filling me, and I moaned. Perfect. The waves receded, leaving me in the wake of his movements.

He gripped my hips, dragging me toward him as he thrust twice. He stilled inside of me on the third time. He roared like the king of his pride, as his own release unleashed from within him.

I crumpled forward, resting my head on the couch cushions, chasing after air. Quietly, he slipped from my body and pressed kisses to my back. His lips touched every bite mark, every scratch before he stood up and patted my ass.

"Stay here, like this," he ordered and then disappeared. I checked over my shoulder and noticed him walking into the bathroom. His back was bare but not smooth. Two long white scars crossed his shoulder blades.

A reminder.

This man didn't come from a gentle part of the world, and he didn't live anywhere near peace.

When he returned from the bathroom, he had a white washcloth in his hand. I let him bathe me, wiping his essence from my thighs and my pussy.

"Get in bed, darlin'." He patted my cheeks again and returned to the bathroom.

I stood up and watched him moving, watched the muscles in his body pull and push his limbs.

"What are you doing?" he asked when he came back to the living room and found me still in the same spot.

"Who hurt you?" The question popped free of my mouth before I could filter it.

A blank slate formed over his expression. He wasn't going to answer me.

"Bedtime, darlin'." He walked past me to the bedroom behind the sliding doors. "Come here, Cherise," he called when I still hadn't followed.

There was more here. More to him. More to us. But he'd put that wall around himself for the night. Maybe I could breach it at dawn.

I climbed into bed with the softest sheets I'd ever

felt in my life. I practically melted into them, and when he pulled the comforter up over us, I moaned.

He chuckled.

"Do you have any idea what sort of heaven this is?" I asked, rolling to my side and staring at him. He was on his back, hands tucked beneath his head.

He turned his head to face me, a smile hinted on his lips. "Yeah. I think I do." He rolled over to his side and kissed my forehead. "Now, go to sleep, angel."

DUSTAN

Cherise found the private jet I brought her to in the morning impressive. Unless her slack jaw and wide eyes while she explored the cabin were indications otherwise. I watched her appreciation for the things I'd begun to take for granted years ago with a hidden grin. I took my seat but let her wander around until the captain came back to inform me, we were getting ready to depart.

"Darlin', you have to sit, or they can't take off." I pointed to the leather captain's chair facing me. I'd rather have her beside me, where I could feel her leg brush mine during the flight or touching her hand or her hair wouldn't take more than a slight movement, but we needed to talk. And talks like that were best done face-to-face.

"Why do you say that?" She straightened up from the minibar she'd been inspecting and made her way toward her seat.

"Say what?" I asked, shrugging out of my jacket and laying it on the seat beside me. Our flight attendant, a tall, pretty brunette with false eyelashes snatched it up right away to hang it in a closet somewhere.

Cherise snapped her seat belt in place. "Darlin'. You have a Chicago accent. Isn't that more of a Southern word?" She tugged her sweater down to cover her hands.

"Just a word I like," I answered. "Fits you." And it did. No matter how fierce she was, how much stronger she could be, she would always have a sweet interior that could be used against her—or me.

She sighed, as though she wasn't really listening to

me and leaned to her left to look down the aisle.

"Nervous?" I asked, reaching across the table separating us and touching her balled-up hands.

"I've flown before," she answered, and turned in the other direction to look out the window. "Not like this, obviously."

I smiled. "Obviously."

"There's a bedroom back there." She jerked a thumb over her shoulder.

"I know." I nodded.

"And Arthur just let you borrow this?" she asked for the third time since we'd driven away from the estate that morning.

"That's what it's for. He has another. Don't worry." I winked.

She sank into her seat, pulling her feet up beneath her and hugging her knees.

"Sir, we'll be taking off now. Is there anything

else you need?" Patricia, our flight attendant, asked, leaning over the empty seat next to me to speak. Her hand rested on my chair with her fingers brushing my hair.

"No. We're fine." I waved her off.

Cherise's narrowed gaze settled on Patricia. I half expected a smart-ass remark to come flying out, but Patricia left unscathed.

"She's handsy," Cherise commented once Patricia was out of hearing range.

"She is," I agreed, enjoying the little pink blossoms bursting on her cheeks.

As the plane made its way down the runway, readying to take off, Cherise's hands came out of her sweatshirt and gripped the table. She shut her eyes and pressed her head back against the chair.

"We'll be in the air in a minute," I said calmly. She just nodded. Her lips pressed together in a thin line, and her nostrils flared as she took deep breaths until the plane finally lifted and began its ascent.

Once we leveled off and she adjusted to the sensation, she opened her eyes and started to relax.

"I don't like the takeoffs. Or the landings," she said with a weak smile. "Not a huge fan of the flying, either."

I laughed. "It would take us two days driving in the car."

"You still haven't told me where exactly we're going and why. And you didn't tell me what you found out last night. What made you so tense when you came back to the room," she pushed.

"I was right about your family farm…it's still yours. And it's bigger than you thought." I pressed my shoulder blades back into my chair and began to unleash all the information Arthur had given me. Every bit of it affected her. It was her family, her situation, and she had every right and every reason to know it all. I held nothing back, not even Bobby's betrayal.

"My father was growing for the Merde family?" she asked the question softly, like just saying the words out loud might give them more weight than she could hold.

"Yes, but it looks like it was a small part of his business. Most of it was completely legitimate, but your uncle saw the potential for more."

"And he killed my family for it," she whispered. Tears built in her eyes, and I cursed the fucking table blocking me from getting to her. I should have had her closer to me.

"So, if the land is mine now, what do I do?" she asked, lifting her gaze to meet mine. She flicked away the tears.

"You have options," I began. "You can take over the farm. You can deal with the Merde family on your own."

"Grow poppies for a drug cartel?" she asked with wide eyes.

"Not the choice I want for you, but it is your choice. We have to take out your uncle though. No other way that would happen." I flattened my hands on the table. Taking out her uncle seemed like a good idea regardless.

"My uncle." She touched the tips of her fingers to her bottom lip. "He…" She exhaled hard. "He was an asshole before my parents' death. When he *suggested* I get out of Minnesota, I couldn't pack fast enough." She had some unleashing of her own to do.

"He hurt you," I said with a hard tone.

"He was an ass. He caught me eavesdropping once when I was kid. He'd come over late and was talking with my father. They got into an argument and woke me up. I went to see what was going on. I don't remember what they fought about. I was only five or six at the time. But I remember being scared of his voice."

I kept my silence, letting her get out whatever she needed.

"But he found me. He was mad, really mad at my dad. My father had already stormed out the back door; my mom was asleep. He grabbed me, shook me so hard my neck felt like it was going to snap. He dragged me to the pantry in the kitchen and threw me inside."

"He locked it," I added, understanding her panic back at my house much better now.

She nodded. "Blocked the door so I couldn't open it. My mom found me in the morning."

"What did she do?"

"She told me to keep away from him, and she told my father."

"Who did nothing?"

Her gaze flashed from her hands to me. "No, not nothing. As much as he could. I think he was scared of his brother, too."

"Your uncle ever do that again?" My decision on her uncle's fate was sealed the second she began this story.

She nodded. "Once he realized how scared I'd been, how upset it had made my father. He locked me in the pantry or a closet whenever he caught me without my parents. Said it was to teach me strength." She scratched her forehead. "I think he just liked tormenting me."

My jaw clenched. I'd heard a similar statement in my life.

"And your father didn't stop him from coming around?"

"It makes sense to me now." She lifted one

shoulder. "My uncle was always talking about setting up meetings and talking to people for my father. I think he was dad's connection to the Merde family. He was the go-between."

I inhaled slowly. Her father's fear of his brother mixed with his inability to handle his own business had put his daughter in danger.

"He's not the go-between anymore," I said. "He's taken over and expanded. That entire field on the other side of that tree line I showed you is full. He's the largest grower in the Midwest."

"And the Merde family isn't going like me walking away from that." She rubbed the heels of her hands on her temples. "Can't I just give them the fields?"

"They won't want that sort of risk. Their growers take the risk of legal trouble if the law can't be bought or controlled. They need the middleman, and right now your uncle is doing a damn fine job."

She growled and smacked the table. "I just wanted to go out for a night! I'm going to find that fucking author and kick her ass."

It took me a second to catch up to her thinking. "The book? You're blaming this all on the book?"

"If I hadn't read it, if I had just stayed low, inside my damn shell, none of this would have happened."

I slid out of my seat and moved to sit beside her. Unbuckling her, I shifted her from her chair to my lap and leaned us back until I cradled her.

"That book was stupid. I'll give you that. But this is your uncle's fault."

"Why didn't he just kill me? He could have had all of the land, and none of this would be happening."

I held her tighter. "You'd be dead," I pointed out.

She snorted.

Anger boiled up inside me.

I pinched her hip and shoved her away from my

chest, capturing her chin in my hand.

She winced at the severity of my grip, but I didn't care.

"If he'd killed you after you survived the fire, it would have looked too suspicious. It would have brought heat to the farm and then possibly the Merde family. That's why he left you alone. But now he's not leaving you alone. Now he wants you dead. And that's a big fucking problem."

Her eyes searched mine.

"I didn't mean…" she whispered. "I didn't mean anything by it."

"You have decisions to make." I released her, the anger fading away with her softness.

She wiggled around to straddle my lap and framed my face with her hands. She held firm.

"My uncle killed my parents." Her eyes darkened, any residual fear lingering from past hurts hidden by the storm of rage. "He dies for that."

"The farm?" I pressed.

"I'm not getting into bed with a cartel." She laughed. "It's bad enough I've gotten into bed with an assassin."

My lips kicked up in a grin. Her cheek was back. "So?"

"My uncle has to have someone helping him, or a rival. Someone who will want the land, want to be top dog."

"Top dog?" I laughed.

"Yeah." She nodded with a smile. "We find out who that is and make him an offer. They can buy me out of the land, and I'll walk away."

I gripped her wrists and pulled her away from my face, planting kisses to each palm before placing them on her knees.

"You want me to kill your uncle?" I asked softly,

pressing a kiss to her neck.

"No."

I pulled back, confused.

"I want to kill my uncle."

I stared at her, in awe and amusement at her bravado, her fierceness. She'd always had it, that didn't surprise me, but see it blossom right before me, in my arms after everything I'd put her through. It took me a moment to react.

"Then I'd better teach you."

CHERISE

I must have lost my mind somewhere between Chicago and New Orleans because I found the idea of Dustan teaching me how to kill a man appealing. Maybe it was because the specific man was Uncle Randy, the man responsible for my parents' death. The man who wanted me dead.

As much as I didn't like flying, the private jet made the experience easier to handle. It didn't hurt that I spent most of the flight either in Dustan's lap or beside him with his hand resting on my leg.

I still didn't like the landing, even with Dustan gripping my hand and assuring me it was fine. But I'd forgotten all about it once I saw the car waiting for us on the tarmac. A sapphire-blue Porsche.

"Arthur's?" I had asked when he opened the passenger door for me.

He shook his head. "No, this is all mine." He grinned like a boy showing off his favorite toy.

"This is a 2020 Porsche 911 coupe. It only just came out." I ran my hands over the dash, feeling his shocked stare on me. "What?"

"You know cars?" He dropped his chin.

I held my stare for only a brief moment before laughing. "I don't know a thing about cars. A patient that comes into the clinic a lot owns a shop. He deals with these types of cars all the time and tries to impress me with all his knowledge. He has a huge crush on this one and showed me at least a dozen pictures of the one he has in his shop."

I clicked my seat belt in place and looked up at him. His dark stare was back.

"He ever ask you out?"

"Like on a date?" I asked with a laugh.

"Yeah, a date." He fired up the engine and peeled away from the plane before I answered.

"Once or twice. But I don't date patients… Dustan, slow down." I pressed my hands to the dash.

He switched gears and took a hard-right turn onto the main stretch of road and out of the airport.

"What's he look like?" Dustan asked, switching gears with ease.

"Why?"

He shot me a dark look. "Answer me."

"Short black hair, like real short. Almost shaved. He's tall, skinny." I tried to recall what he looked like. "I don't know, normal. He just looked normal."

"Name?" Dustan sped up. I braced myself against the dash and the door with my hands.

"I can't—"

"Name!" he yelled.

"John Smith," I snapped.

He laughed. Not a funny that's a funny joke laugh, but a deep-rooted, sinister sound that set the hairs on the back of my neck on edge.

"John fucking Smith." He nodded and took another turn down a narrow dirt road.

"Dustan, slow down. Please," I begged. In addition to the fear of hitting a ditch and taking a fatal roll in the car, I picked up on his fevered irritation. Something I'd said pissed him off.

"His name isn't John Smith." He shook his head and hit the gas more as we came up to a secluded stretch of trees. "It's such an obvious alias it's not obvious," he said, but it sounded like a one-man conversation, so I kept silent. Watching the trees swish past the window kept me occupied, and my heart thumping in my chest.

"What are you talking about?" I shouted as he

took another sharp turn. "Dustan!"

After the turn, he slammed on the brakes and brought the car to a skidded stop, kicking up dust all around us, coming within inches of the gate. He twisted in his seat to look at me. The thundering of my heart beating in my ears slowed down more the longer he kept me pinned beneath his stare.

"John Smith owns the only auto body shop on your side of the city that works on cars like this. Isn't that right?" But he wasn't asking me, he just kept talking. "He has a scar, right here—" he pointed to the spot just below his left eye. "And he wears a diamond stud in both ears."

Confusion swished through my mind. "You know him."

"John Smith is Robert Cantino." He paused a beat. "Bobby."

"Your Bobby?" I asked, but I didn't need to, not

really. What I really needed to do was down a bottle of wine.

"Yeah. My Bobby. How long has he been coming into your office?"

"For the last month, I think."

He nodded and turned back around, hitting some buttons on his phone until the gate swung open. I watched him while he focused on the entrance. The little tic in his jaw was back.

"He was there for the Merde family. Watching me," I said after too-dead air piled between us.

We drove forward. "Sounds like it."

I watched the gate shut behind us in the sideview mirror. Thinking back, I tried to recall anything out of the ordinary about John/Bobby.

"He couldn't have known I'd run into you at that bar." I squeezed my eyes closed. "Right? He couldn't have set me up to run into you. And even if he had, he wouldn't have known I'd see you—see what you did—" The familiar bubbles of panic compounded inside me, sucking the air from my lungs and kicking my heart into overdrive.

Exactly how many things in my life were real? Was any of it? Was I ever at any point in control of one single moment of my life?

"Bobby's a resourceful guy. But it doesn't matter what he planned or what he did. The bottom line is he betrayed me." Dustan didn't trust many people, I could sense that, but he had trusted Bobby. And to have that sort of bond snapped by betrayal—it had to cut him deep.

I licked my lips and pressed my body back into my seat. He drove at a more reasonable pace up a winding trail, through more clumps of trees until the road brought us to a house. A light-blue farmhouse with a wraparound porch.

It reminded me of home, and for the first time in years I let myself feel the hurt, the homesickness I'd been pushing down. With the car parked, I popped open my door and climbed out, staring at the porch swing. Memories of my mother sitting on the one back home with me, flipping through the teen magazines she'd bring me from the store bombarded me.

If a house similar to my childhood home could bring out so much pain, what would it be like when I set foot in my actual house. Would I be able to see around the ache and do what needed to be done?

"Hey, darlin'. You okay?" Dustan's hands settled on my shoulders.

I sucked in a breath, shoving the hurt back behind the edge, and nodded. "Yeah. How many houses do you actually own?" I forced some levity to my voice, but when I turned to look at him, I could see how miserably I'd failed.

He brushed my hair from my face, tucking it behind my ears.

"This is all going to work out fine. I swear it." I could sense the determination in him. He wanted me to believe him.

"Since when are you in the happily-ever-after business?" I asked and pulled away turning and headed for the house.

He didn't stop me or contradict me. The trunk of the car slammed, and his heavy footsteps clunked up the stairs a few moments later. I stood at the door with my hands tucked in the sleeves of my sweater, waiting for him to open the door.

"Will we have company here, too?" I asked.

He shoved a key into the lock on the door and shook his head. "No. Bobby doesn't know the location of this house. No one does."

"Not even Arthur?"

He gave me a side look like my tone hit a nerve. Maybe the smart-ass in me was coming back.

"Get inside, darlin', before you catch yourself some trouble." He winked and pushed the door open.

I brushed past him into the house, flashing him a grin of my own. I would deal with everything soon enough. My uncle, the farm, the Merde family, all of it. But right now, I just wanted to forget that and find a sandwich.

DUSTAN

I found Cherise standing in my living room, staring at the television screen. I'd left her on her own since we arrived at my estate, letting her wander around and get her bearings in order. When she'd seen the house, something had come over her. I knew the horrified expression, had seen it with men I knew who came home from the same deployments.

One look at their families, at something familiar, and the memories of their past hurtled at them—knocking them off-kilter. Having your feet on solid ground isn't as easy when everything you've been locking up comes flying out at you. It catches you off guard, and when Cherise took in the farmhouse, the same had been done to her.

I chose this house because it was the closest of my safe houses to her uncle. She'd reacted to this place, and I knew it only would have been worse if she'd been at her childhood home. I'd given her space to let her mind get back under her control, but we needed to get out to the range before the sun began to set.

"Cherise, what are you watching?" I asked, rounding the couch to get a better view of the screen.

The news reporter was discussing the latest reports of overdose victims in the country.

"Opioids. Those come from poppy plants, right?" she asked without moving her gaze to me.

"Yeah." I gently took the remote from her hand and flicked the show off. "It's used to make heroine, but you already know that."

Her cheeks puffed out, and she slid her hands into the ass pockets of her jeans. I'd been able to grab her enough clothes to last at least another week while were in New Orleans, and the way those jeans hugged her ass and hips, I would be fine if she kept herself in them every day.

"How can those fields you showed me go undetected?" she asked.

I shrugged. "Dirty law enforcement. How much do you know about the police department in your town?"

"Not much. Mom had the sheriff over for dinner a few times, but I didn't join them."

"Right." I pointed a finger at her. "He's probably getting quite the payday from your uncle to look the other way and give him any leads as to the DEA sniffing around. Your town is a tiny blip on the map, not really a hot spot for drug cartels or poppy growers."

She inhaled a long breath. "So complicated."

"To the innocent, yeah." I laughed. "C'mon out

back. Time for your lesson." I gestured for her to follow me and headed through the living room and toward the rear of the house.

"Don't we need safety glasses or something?" she asked as she stepped off the porch.

I raised my eyebrows. "Safety glasses?"

Her cheeks erupted red, and she laughed. "That was stupid. I—I'm nervous is all."

"It's just a gun." I held up the Glock 19 I brought out for her lesson. "It's not even loaded yet."

Her eyes focused on the pistol in my hand, and the bright-red blush drained away. "Right."

"You don't have to do this if you don't want. I can—"

"No. I can do it." She gave a firm nod. "I can."

I understood the need she had to regain power in her life, but I also knew what would happen after she pointed her gun at her uncle. Nothing would be the same. There was no going back from the act. She'd be forever changed.

And I wasn't positive I wanted her any different than she was.

"Okay." I cradled the gun in my palm. "This here's the barrel, this is the magazine well, your front sight alignment, and your rear alignment." I looked up at her. "The trigger seems self-explanatory."

She kept her focus on my hand and didn't give me a second glance.

"When you hold the gun, you wrap your trigger hand around the magazine well and press your finger along the barrel. Do not touch the trigger unless you're going to use it. If you're just aiming, you keep your finger along here. Got it?" I positioned my hand the way I wanted her to memorize holding it.

"Got it. Palm here and finger there." She ran her finger along the barrel.

"When you take aim, don't look at your target to aim. You look here at the front sight." I tapped the tag on the front of the barrel. You line this up with your target and then make sure this back alignment, these two pieces"—I pointed to the rear of the barrel—"are in alignment with the front."

"So, like a football goal post?" she asked, leaning farther toward me to see better.

"Yeah." I grinned. "Sorta like that."

I handed her the Glock. "Go ahead. It's not loaded. Once you have the positioning right, I'll give you a live magazine."

She held the gun, feeling the weight in her palm before wrapping her hand around the back strap and around the grip, lifting it away from her. Pointing at a nearby tree, she adjusted her arms until the alignment was how she wanted it.

"Use your other hand to steady yourself." I

brought up her left arm and took her hand. "Your pointer finger should be right beneath the trigger guard. While your right hand is pushing the gun out, your left hand pulls it back in. You'll have more stability that way. Don't lock your arms." I pressed on her elbows. "It causes fatigue faster."

"Okay." She blinked hard. "No locking my arms."

"Good. Good position." I stepped away to check her stance. Natural. "Now, wrap your finger around the trigger."

"The tip of my finger?" she asked.

"Just do it naturally, don't think too hard on it." I folded my arms over my chest. "Okay, now squeeze the trigger."

She squeezed the trigger until the magazine clicked off the empty round. She blew out a loud breath and dropped her hands.

"After you shoot, follow through. Don't drop

your arms right away."

"What if he shoots back?" she asked, like the idea had just occurred to her that she might not be the only one armed.

"I'll be there covering you. Don't worry about that."

"But you don't shoot him," she said, whipping around to face me.

"No. I won't," I agreed. "It's yours, but I'll be there in case it goes bad."

Her shoulders dropped, and the tension eased out of her body. "Can I try a real shot?"

I took the gun from her and pulled the loaded magazine from my back pocket. Showing her how, I released the empty magazine clip and reloaded it with the live rounds. I made sure the safety was on and handed it to her.

"How do you know I won't use this against you?"

she asked, keeping it pointed at the ground at her side.

"I don't," I said with firmness. "My part in all of this is up to you. If you want to point that at me and walk away, you won't have me chasing you."

Her eyes softened; a gentle sadness bloomed.

"Those people my uncle sent after me. They'd be chasing me," she said softly.

"Yes. They won't stop until they are stopped or you're dead." It was the truth, as much as I could see it hurt her to hear it, I wasn't going to sugarcoat it. I'd already lied when I told her I wouldn't chase her. I wouldn't stretch the truth any more than that.

"I wasn't really thinking to use—"

"I know." I enjoyed the pink resurface on her cheeks. "Let's go over to those trees there. One of them is starting to die anyway. You can kill it for me." I pointed to the area I wanted, and she led the way.

Once we were close enough, she stopped and

checked with me about the range. I nodded and moved to her right. "I'll stand here." Far enough behind and to the side to be safe but still watch her form.

She was a quick study, my girl. She held all of her positioning correctly and took a natural stance. When she took the shot, the kickback gave her minimal trouble. A chunk of tree bark flew off, and she kept her aim for a few moments before slowly lowering the gun and putting the safety on.

"Did you hit where you wanted?" I asked, holding my applause. She'd done better than most men I'd seen pick up a gun in basic training. She mouthed to herself all the instructions I'd given her and done brilliantly.

"It hit a little low. Can I try again?" She was already aiming.

"Make sure you watch your front alignment once you're lined up. When you pull the trigger, hold steady. If you hit low, it's because you jerked downward when you shot."

She nodded, letting me know she'd heard me, and then lined herself up again.

"Go ahead," I said, watching the tree.

The shot rang out, and another chunk flew off, inches above the first hit.

She shot me a grin.

"Go ahead," I said, waving my hand, knowing what she wanted. "Finish the magazine."

I could swear I heard her giggle, but I knew she'd deny it. Cherise wasn't a giggle sort of girl. It was a natural fit with how she held herself with the weapon, how pleased she was when she hit her target a second and third time. I couldn't help but grin with each shot, and each time her smile got wider and wider.

I was going to have to let her keep that one. That gun was hers.

And she was quickly becoming mine.

Whether we wanted it or not.

CHERISE

Dustan walked through the bedroom, a pair of boxers hanging low on his hips. I watched from my hiding spot beneath the covers as his body moved, all the muscles going taut and relaxing with each motion. The moments of fear seemed so long in the past, I wasn't sure I could see them clearly anymore.

The bruise on my chin was already fading into a yellow mess, and the welts covering my ass were healing. We'd been at his house, tucked away from everyone, for four days. Each morning was the same. He got out of bed early, went for a run, and hit the shower before I even opened my eyes.

After breakfast, he'd give me his guns—never

Simone—and let me out back to blow off a chunk of a tree trunk. My aim improved, but still, when I pictured blood pouring out of the wound, when I heard in my mind a cry of pain, I wasn't sure I had the strength to squeeze the trigger when it came time.

"I see you gawking at me," Dustan said with his back to me while he dug around a drawer.

"I don't gawk," I protested, and shoved the blanket down and sat up. "I appreciate."

He craned his neck to shoot me a look over his shoulder. When had these mornings become so easy?

"Well, appreciate while you're getting dressed. We're leaving this afternoon."

The lightness of my soul evaporated, and a boulder dropped inside.

"Where?" I pulled my feet toward my ass and hugged my knees.

He slipped an undershirt over his head and faced

me. "To your uncle's. It's a long drive, so we'll get there at night. We'll stay at a motel up there and, in the morning, I'll make contact."

His manner was so businesslike. We might have been discussing purchasing a new storefront for a chain. Resting my elbow on my knee, I cradled my head in my hand. I needed a cup of coffee before I dealt with family betrayals and drug cartels.

"And what about me? You aren't taking out my uncle. You said—"

"I know what I said, darlin'." He dropped his chin and settled his cautionary glare on me. "You'll be with me every step of the way. But you start getting your attitude riled up, and you'll be walking a little less ladylike."

I scoffed. "When did I ever walk ladylike?"

His lips spread into a wide grin, showcasing that sexy crease on the side of his mouth. "I suppose not.

You have more of a girl swagger." He winked and went back to finding his pants.

"Is there coffee?" I swung my legs over the side of the bed. Dustan had a surprising amount of supplies at his house. Most of the food was unperishable, but he'd made a run to a grocery store to get a few things of necessity. Like real cream for my coffee. The powdered stuff wouldn't cut it.

"Just turned on the pot when I got back." He put his foot up on the bed to lace up his boots. "Don't take too long sitting with your coffee. I want you to take one more practice run out at the tree. I put up an actual target for you out there this morning."

I nodded. "Sure. Where are you going?" I asked.

"I'll be in my office. Need to check in and get some intel then, after lunch, we'll head out."

"Bobby?" I asked quietly, approaching the subject with as much caution as possible. A twitch of his jaw gave him away, but it faded after only a second.

"Nothing yet. But he's not stupid. After that asshole failed to get you before, Bobby would figure I made him. He's one of only two people who know where that house is."

"The other being Arthur."

He nodded. "Small cup of coffee then outside."

"At some point, you have to stop bossing me around." I slipped off the bed and tugged my T-shirt down around my ass. I'd lost my panties somewhere in the bedding during the night when Dustan slid his hands into the elastic and pushed them down. I would have been irritated at being awakened in the middle of the night, but his mouth apologized in all the right ways.

"Why's that?" he asked from the doorway.

"Well, once this is all over and I go home—you won't have me to boss around anymore," I said lightly, as though the idea of being separated from him wouldn't faze me in the least. Because that's how it needed to be.

Playing house the past few days was sweet. We'd had fun and fuck if he didn't make my panties melt off with a simple flick of his eyebrow. But his life and mine didn't meld together well. Aside from the fact he had kidnaped me. A fact my mind kept sweeping into a far corner.

His gaze dropped while the tension in his shoulders pulled his posture back. "Coffee." He tapped the doorjamb then disappeared into the hall. His footsteps faded down the stairs.

During my shower and my small cup of coffee, I reminded myself of all the reasons my uncle deserved what was coming toward him. He'd killed my parents and had tried to kill me. He'd sent men after me. He'd stolen my childhood home. He'd tormented me as a child and bullied me as an adult.

Yet, when I stood in the yard with the gun in my hand, my finger wrapped tightly around the trigger, and I stared at his picture Dustan had put up on the tree, I hesitated.

True, my uncle had done all those things. He was rotted from the inside out, but if I did this, if I took his life, would I be planting a dying seed inside me as well?

Did I really have what it took to end a life, even one as soulless as his?

"You're breathing is too erratic." Dustan startled me. I pulled my finger from the trigger and turned to face him.

His arms were crossed over his chest as he stood ten feet behind me.

"I can see from here your shoulders and back are moving because of your breath. You have to slow it down or it will jerk your shot." He looked at his watch then at the target. "Not even one round yet."

I'd been staring at my uncle's mug for over half an hour already and not one shot had been taken.

"I can do this," I argued, even if he hadn't said anything to the contrary, I could hear his doubt. I knew he didn't think I had it in me, and a man like him would know.

"I didn't say you couldn't." He shrugged and walked toward me. "Get back in your stance." He waved a hand at me.

I repositioned myself and the gun, aiming at the target again. His nose. If I aimed for his nose, it wasn't so clear about his identity. Or that's what I told myself. I was pretty convincing, too.

"Okay, now, slowly inhale." He got closer to me but didn't touch me. "With me, ready?"

I nodded.

"Slow, darlin'." I followed his cue.

I lined up the front sight with the nose and went back to focusing on the sound and feel of Dustan's breath near my ear.

"Finger on the trigger," he instructed softly. "Good girl. Whenever you're ready."

Backsights aligned, nose in view, breathing steady and even. I squeezed. I stumbled back a step but kept my aim, followed through with the shot and quickly found where I'd hit.

Uncle Randy's nose was nowhere to be seen.

"Excellent." Dustan congratulated me but still kept his hands off. "Again."

I repositioned. The feel of the gun firing in my hand quickly became second nature. Dustan had had me fire off four magazines a day since he'd started my lessons. The kickback didn't startle me anymore, and the loud pop of the shot became background noise.

I squeezed off another round, and another until the last bullet left the chamber and the magazine was empty. Only then did Dustan step forward and touch me. He placed a hand on my shoulder to get my attention then offered another loaded magazine.

I took it, reloading the gun how he'd shown me and racked the slider back to start again. Once I was positioned, he tapped my shoulder.

"Not the tree." He pointed to the left of it. "There's a deer."

I swallowed. "You want me to kill the deer?"

"It won't go to waste. We'll take it with us, and I'll drop it with someone who'll use it." His brows lowered.

I tapped my teeth together, thinking, letting the idea rattle around my brain. A life. I'd be taking a life, and I needed to get my heart used to the idea.

I nodded and moved my aim toward Bambi. My

target lined up with its chest. Would that do it clean? Or would I have to hit it twice?

My heart hammered; my breath picked up no matter how much I tried to slow it down. The deer's ears twitched while it munched down on some grass.

The sound of my own panting deafened me as moments ticked by without movement from me. I touched the trigger, pushing myself to do what I needed to do. To get through this test. Because that's what it was. If not for Dustan, for myself.

The deer raised its head and turned toward us, still chewing. I swallowed. My aim moved now to the head. A cleaner shot. Faster death.

"Fuck!" I moaned and dropped my arms. The deer trotted off unscathed and unknowing of how close it came to death.

"It's okay." Dustan removed the gun from my hand and released the slide. "Let's get some food before we hit the road." He tugged on my arm.

"I can do it, Dustan," I said again, angry with myself and with him for doubting me. I could sense it. I knew it was lingering in his mind that I didn't have it in me.

He stopped walking and lifted my chin with his fist. "Still didn't say you couldn't," he said.

"You think it."

"I think you'll do what's right when the time comes. It's who you are. Doing the right thing."

"I'm not that good," I defended.

He laughed. "I never said doing the right thing was a good thing."

"You confuse me."

He brushed a kiss over my lips, soft and tender, muddling my tense thoughts even more. "Good. You're cute when you're confused."

"And when I'm scared?" I asked quietly, the small

ball of fear for the next day bouncing steadily in my stomach.

"When you're afraid of me? Of what I'm going to do to you, how hard I'm going to fuck you or spank you…you're sexy as hell."

The ball of fear rolled off to the side, and desire built up in me. No number of touches from Dustan were enough, I always craved another.

"And right now?" I asked, narrowing my eyelids.

"Right now, I'm going to feed you a sandwich and strap you into the car." He winked and stepped back. "There'll be enough time for the rest when we get to the motel tonight."

I took a deep breath and tried to play like his teasing didn't affect me. But I should have known better.

"Whatever." I rolled my eyes, earning a sharp smack to my ass. When I spun around to him, he grabbed my shoulders and kissed the snark right out of me.

I softened beneath his strength, pressing my hands to his chest, feeling his muscles, his tension, and melting into it. A hand wrapped around my neck, holding me firmly when he pulled back.

"You're going to be fine. You'll do fine, and if at any time you need me—you ask. All right, darlin'?" His questions were rushed, like if he didn't get them out fast enough, I'd change topics on him.

"Yeah, Dustan. I know." I nodded, curling my fingers into his shirt.

"Good." He kissed the tip of my nose, the gentlest gesture he'd ever given me, and smacked my ass again. "Sandwich." He let me go and walked ahead of me to the house, not looking back to see if I was following.

He didn't need to.

He already knew I would be only a few steps

behind him.

Following where he led.

DUSTAN

A heavy cigar smell clung to the air in the motel room, but Cherise didn't complain. Her nose scrunched up when we walked in, but she kept her opinion about it to herself. She'd been quiet nearly the entire drive.

"I need a shower." She dropped her bag on one of the queen beds. "A hot bath would be amazing. Do you think there's a tub?" she asked, rolling her head from one side to the other.

I peeked inside the washroom, standard tub and toilet. Clean. "There's a tub, but not sure how relaxing it will be."

She heaved a sigh and dug out a T-shirt from the bag. Her nightgown. I intentionally hadn't gotten her any pajama-type clothes, but apparently, she was used to sleeping in T-shirts because she never questioned it.

"Hot shower will have to do." She balled up the shirt in her hand.

"I'll order some food," I offered, picking up the local take-out menu left by the telephone.

"I'm not really hungry," she said and breezed past me into the bathroom, shutting the door softly once inside.

Not hungry. She had barely touched her sandwich before we left and hadn't eaten anything while we were driving. Her nerves were getting the best of her. Tomorrow was going to be a dark day in her life, and I knew dark.

I ordered a small cheese pizza with a side salad and some sodas then checked on Cherise. I pushed the door open enough to hear the water running and her gentle hum.

Satisfied she'd be occupied for the next few minutes, I pulled up the contact information Arthur sent me a few hours ago and dialed. A rough-sounding voice answered the phone.

"I have it." The gruff voice answered my question before I asked it. I went to the window and pushed the curtain to the side with my fingers, checking the parking lot below.

"Good. You know where to bring it?" I asked, eyeing a car pulling into the lot. A grey minivan parked two spots down from our door, and a gaggle of kids dressed in soccer uniforms and laughing bounded out the side doors.

"Yeah. Send me the time, and I'll be there."

A man looking proud and worn out climbed out of the driver's side, and he motioned for the woman to come around the car. He wrapped his arm around her, pulling her to his side for a kiss before following the kids off to their room.

"Will do." I clicked off the call. I leaned forward a bit, trying to catch another glimpse of the couple, but they'd strolled beneath the walkway out of sight. As tired as they both looked, when he'd touched her, she'd lit up for him. A simple kiss to her head, and they'd both seemed to have melted into each other.

"What's so interesting out there?" Cherise's soft voice carried through the motel room. I dropped the curtain and faced her, taking in her sweetness.

Droplets of water clung to her shoulders from the ends of her hair brushing along them. I walked to her and grasped her chin, eliciting a small gasp. She was even sweeter when I caught her off guard.

I turned her face. "This bruise is finally starting to fade." I ran my thumb over the discolored flesh. I didn't regret my actions—at the time they were warranted, but I didn't like seeing the evidence of it every damn time I looked at her.

"Turn around so I can see your ass." I knew I was being rough. I couldn't help it when it came to her. Gentle didn't suit her, and it sure as fuck never suited me.

I spun her around, ripping the towel from her body as she moved.

"Dustan." She put her hands up against the wall when I pressed her to it; she twisted to look at me over her shoulder.

I flattened my hand between her shoulder blades, keeping her against the wall so I could get a good look at her ass without any interruptions. The welts had eased, and only two small yellowish-purple splotches remained as evidence of her prior whippings. My fingertips skated across her skin, her perfectly smooth, creamy skin.

The image of the couple popped into my mind.

I tilted back to look up at her, to see her expression. Her tongue touched her top lip. Her pupils large and round, knocking out the milk-chocolate coloring of her eyes. She was lit up. For me.

I smacked her ass, grinning at her little jump of surprise. "On the bed," I ordered and released her. She scrambled onto it, not bothering to grab for the towel that lay at her feet.

She scooted on the mattress until her back pressed against the headboard; her gaze roaming over my body as I moved toward her. I stripped out of my clothes, not being smooth or seductive about the affair. I just needed my skin against hers.

I slid onto the bed, grabbing her ankles and jerking them toward me until she was flat beneath me. Stretching out over her body, I pressed myself against her.

Fuck, she felt good. Warm and right. This woman

felt right.

I propped myself on my elbows, looking down at her face. Her eyes were wide and searching me, but she didn't speak. I wiped away the wet strands of hair from her face and kissed her cheeks. I planted kisses on the bruise I'd given her, the closest to an apology she'd ever get for me on that topic. Then I took her mouth.

Her arms wrapped around my back, holding me tight to her. She nipped at my lip, and I licked her back. Pure animal instinct drove us.

I slid my hand over her body, down to her hip then between us until I found her pussy. Hot and wet, ready for me. Such a good fucking girl. I thrust two fingers into her, taking her cry into my mouth when I curled them, finding that secret button of hers.

"Fuck, Dustan," she muttered against my lips.

"Soon, darlin'. First, I want you to shatter for me."

I thrust again, harder, and used the heel of my palm to rub against her clit.

Her fingers dug into my shoulders, and she arched her back, pushing her hips up at me.

Her eyes slammed shut; her mouth dropped open in the perfect gasp.

"That's it, darlin', give me what I want," I whispered in her ear, licking her earlobe before biting down.

"Fuck!" She moaned with the little bite of pain and panted harder when I thrust a third finger inside her tight, hot pussy.

"So good for me." I kissed her cheek. "So good." I bit down on her neck.

A shudder ran through her body. I felt ever bit of it, every little tremble, every jerk of her muscles as her orgasm built.

"You want to be good for me, right, darlin'? You want to be my good girl?" I grazed my teeth along her jaw.

"Yes—" Her words cut off with her scream. I thrust my fingers harder into her pussy.

"That's it, good. Good girl." I cheered her on, knowing she was too wrapped up in her orgasm to hear me. Her pussy clenched around my fingers, but I continued to fuck her with them until the tension eased away from her body and she was left panting and soft beneath me.

"Fuck. That was gorgeous." I kissed her and slipped my hand from between her legs.

Her eyes fluttered open, and she found my gaze. A soft-pink hue covered her cheeks.

"Such a pretty blush." I kissed her again. "Let's see how red we can make that pretty face of yours." I moved over again, covering her with my body as my cock easily found her entrance.

"You're going to come again for me," I instructed

her and lifted her right leg beneath my arm, hooking it and raising it higher.

"I don't think I can." She shook her head, but it only made me more determined. She really should know that about me by now.

"Then you will." I thrust forward. I grunted, unable and unwilling to contain the animalistic sound. Her pussy gripped my cock.

I rocked hard into her, taking her little gasps and cries into my mouth as I fucked harder and harder still. I cradled her face with one hand while my arm pulled her leg up higher.

"Fuck, you're so tight," I groaned.

Her hands roamed over my shoulders, my chest as I continued to thrust into her, each stroke harder than the last.

"Oh!" She gripped my arms, and I knew I had her. Grinding my hips into her with each stroke brought her to the edge with me.

I looked down at her, at her wide eyes, her full lips. So many words crossed my mind, so many things I wanted to say to make the moment last longer, but I pulled them back.

"Dustan!" she screamed out and bucked up at me, her orgasm tearing through her again. Her pussy gripped me harder, the pulsation of her release triggered the loss of my control.

I plowed into her, harder and without any resolve. One stroke then two then I lost myself in her. Our cries of release mingled in the air in the same fashion our bodies melded in the bed.

I pressed my forehead against hers, catching my breath and needing her close to me. I released my hold on her leg and let her stretch beneath me as I slipped from her body. I pushed myself up, sitting back on my heels, and spread her legs wider, watching my seed slide out of her pussy.

"It's okay. I have an IUD. I can't get pregnant," she said.

I shook my head. "It's not that." I ran my middle finger through her folds, collecting the fluid and smearing it over her thigh. "You're mine now, darlin'. Good and truly mine." I reached down from the bed to grab my shirt. "When this is done, we'll figure out the next step, but you're not alone anymore." I wiped her clean, except for her thigh. I wanted my mark to stay on her.

"Dustan," she sighed, but when I looked up at her, she paused a beat. "Come to bed. I'm tired." She pulled the covers down on the empty side of the bed and maneuvered herself between them.

There was a knock on the door.

"Pizza." I pulled on my slacks. "You're eating before you're sleeping," I ordered and went to the door.

"Who was your first kill?" Cherise asked just as I took a sip of my beer.

"What?" I laughed.

"Your first kill. The first target you had. Is that right? Am I saying that right?" She nibbled on the crust of her piece. Having eaten the cheese first then the dough, she was finally at the crust.

I cleared my throat and leaned back in the chair. She'd thrown on a shirt after the pizza was delivered, but she was still naked beneath. Just because she threw some cotton fabric over her body didn't mean I couldn't see it, or feel it, or imagine it.

"Yeah, you said it right." I nodded, tapping my fingers on the beer bottle. Thankfully, the shopette in the lobby had beer. Not the best, but it would do.

"So?" She took a bite. "Who?"

I inhaled slow, studying her. "My dad." Her eyes widened. "And my mom."

"Why?" she asked, taking another bite of crust. The surprise was there, lingering in her gaze, but she'd kept it out of her voice.

"The marks on my back, the ones you asked about are from them. They took me and my sister camping one summer—or at least that's what we thought. It turned out they were hiding from some loan sharks. My dad was hammered, so drunk he could barely stand. He dropped the metal roasting stick he'd been using into the campfire. I made a joke about it." I paused a moment. "I don't remember exactly what I said, but I pissed him off. He picked up the damn thing and hit me across my back with it. The burns left scars."

"How old were you?" she asked.

"Twelve." I sipped my beer. "My sister was only

five. They were too out of it to take care of her, so I did it most of the time. I was able to keep my dad away from her when he was drunk, but when we got older it was harder. I had to pick up a job to help pay the rent so we wouldn't get evicted again, so some nights I wasn't home. She was smart enough to stay out of their way when they got into a fight though. She'd hide in her room until I got home."

"And then you went into the military?" she asked, but not with the accusatory tone I would have expected. If I'd stayed home, things would have been different.

"Yeah. I shouldn't have. I should have been there for her, but I was going to take her with me after my first tour. I was going to set her up on base with me, and we'd be good to go. But—" I closed my eyes and took another pull of my beer. "That didn't happen as planned."

"So, your parents were first." She drifted over the topic of my sister's suicide.

"Yeah." I laughed. "It's how I got my spot in the organization, too. They owed a lot of people money, fucked over a lot of people with power. I'm not really sure how bad it all had gotten, only that they'd gotten themselves in Arthur's crosshairs."

She moved out of her chair and settled herself in my lap, touching her fingers to my forehead.

"And you took the job," she said with a nod.

"Yeah, something like that. After that, I went with him. There's no going back from that." I remembered that night. The blood and the satisfaction. Breathing came easier after I'd pulled the trigger on them, a weight that had been shoving me to my knees my entire life lifted.

"Do you regret it?" she asked wiping her hand along my jaw.

"Only that I didn't do it sooner." I looked up into her eyes, expecting to see a hint of fear but saw nothing.

"Do you regret not killing me in that alley?" she asked, looking down at her lap.

I grabbed her chin and jerked her face toward mine. "That's a fucking stupid question." My voice hardened, as did the rest of me with the words coming from her mouth.

"It's a valid one," she said, not pulling away from me, but meeting me glare for glare.

"I wasn't going to kill you in the alley. Or at your apartment." I gripped her chin harder. "Even if you had gone to the cops, the whole thing would have been handled. I don't kill innocents."

"You acted like you were going to."

I let her chin go.

"You punched me," she said and touched her jaw.

"We needed to go, and you were causing trouble." I pulled her hand from her face and held it to my chest. "Going after you—that was a gut call. But I don't regret it."

She pushed a smile to her lips. "Is it really fucked up that I don't, either?"

I brushed her hair from her eyes. "No. There isn't a fucked-up thing about you."

I got up from my chair, cradling her in my arms, and took us to the bed. "Tomorrow's going to be a long day. You need sleep." I laid her on the bed and untucked the covers for her to climb under.

"Come to bed with me, Dustan." She yawned.

"I'm just going to turn out the lights first."

I checked the door, took another look out at the parking lot, and flipped off the lights in the bathroom. By the time I made my rounds of the five hundred square feet and made it back to the bed, she'd slipped into sleep.

I watched her sleeping, her soft sweetness. Someone like me didn't get to keep gifts like her. I knew it, but I wasn't letting it stop me from climbing beneath the covers and pulling her body against mine.

Where she belonged.

Right or not.

She belonged to me.

CHERISE

The clothes Dustan had gotten for me while we were in New Orleans didn't include a wide variety of underwear. I grabbed the last pair in the bag and pulled them over my ass. All lace. I looked at myself in the mirror, judging the extra padding with a frown. I poked at my cheeks and sighed. I had much bigger problems coming my way, so worrying over the extra five pounds of ass felt like a guilty pleasure.

I finished dressing and shoved my feet into my shoes. Checking the clock radio on the nightstand, I figured I had another ten minutes before Dustan returned from the donut shop across the street. I'd said I wasn't hungry, but he only glared at me, pinched my hip, and told me to stay put while he grabbed donut holes and coffee.

He was probably just trying to get my mind off what was barreling down at us in a few hours, but he had to know donut holes weren't going to work. Feeling the gun staring at me, I picked it up off the dresser. It was heavy in my hand. The weight of my decision added weight to it, I was sure.

I had no doubt my uncle deserved whatever happened to him when we got to the farm; that wasn't even a question. He'd killed my family. But then I remembered how I'd frozen when Dustan told me to kill the deer. I could justify that the deer was innocent and didn't deserve to die, even if we were going to give it to a family for their meat locker. But in my heart, I knew what it was. The moral dilemma of taking a life twisted my gut.

A booming knock jolted me from my

considerations, and I huffed a laugh at myself. I was getting myself all worked up. Donuts were waiting for me. I shoved the gun into my bag.

"Hands too full to open the door?" I called as I made my way. "How many donuts did you buy?" I jerked the door open.

My heart took a nosedive.

"Sorry, Cherise, no donuts." Uncle Randy sneered at me.

"Uncle Randy. Uh, what are you doing here?" I asked, trying to see around his bulky form. Dustan had to be back any second.

"That was my question for you. Since I made it pretty damn clear not to come back." Another man wearing jeans and a black hoodie stepped behind my uncle, looking from one side of the hall to the other.

I stared, slack-jawed. The same tremor of fear trickled through my body as when I was younger. He hadn't changed in the last years. The same slimy sneer perched on the same fat lips. His suit jacket swung open around his belly where the buttons on his shirt were holding firm but losing resolve.

"I think it's best you come home with me, Cherise." He reached a hand toward me. I stepped back on instinct. He sighed and ran his tongue over the front of his top teeth.

"Don't cause a scene," he snapped at me. "I'd rather not have to drag you to the car, but I will." And by *I* he obviously meant the thug hanging out behind him. I couldn't see his face clearly, but if he worked for my uncle, he wasn't going to be on my side.

"Okay. Let me grab my bag." I stepped back another step, hoping he'd follow me inside. If I could keep him in the room, lock his friend outside, Dustan would be back.

Uncle Randy pushed the door open and stayed in

the doorway. His figure blocked out the sunlight.

"We need to go." He waved his hand at me. There was a time limit. He had to know Dustan would be back soon.

"I just need to grab my stuff. I think I left my brush in the—"

"Now, Cherise! No fucking around." His patience thinned. I stilled for a moment, grabbing my bag from the dresser and slinging the strap over my shoulder, hugging it to my chest.

"Okay, okay." I nodded, not raising my eyes to meet his. The little girl inside kicked me, knocking my heart into an erratic beat and pushing the air from my lungs, making it harder to keep a level head.

"Let's go." He grabbed my arm as soon as I stepped within touching range and pulled me out of the room. His goon turned away when I tried to get a look at his face.

Uncle Randy didn't give any more instructions as he pulled me down the stairs and to his car. Another man, a driver, was waiting for us. The hooded helper opened the back door, and my uncle shoved me inside. I crawled to the opposite side of the car, searching through the window for Dustan.

The car jerked into motion, and tears flooded my eyes. I had to get away. I grabbed for the door handle, but the click of the hammer being pulled back on my uncle's pistol froze my hand.

"Just sit nice," he said.

I turned away from the door and looked down at his lap where he held his gun pointed at me. My mouth dried, stopping any words that were forming in my mind. I nodded numbly and sat in the seat, holding my bag to my chest.

The driver flipped on the radio to a country station, and, other than the music, there were no sounds on the ride to my family home. Where I'd grown up and my parents had died.

My uncle had put a gate up at the border of the land. A white iron gate that needed to be unlocked for entry. The driver punched in the code on the little box, and the gates swung open. As the car made its way up the drive, the house came into view.

The fire that killed my parents had destroyed half the house, but my uncle had repaired it. It didn't look different in any way. The same baby-blue coloring, dark-brown window shutters, and the white porch that wrapped around the entire house. Everything was exactly as I remembered it as a child.

After the fire, when I came home for the funerals, the house had been so badly damaged I'd had to stay in a hotel in town. Which suited me fine at the time, as being anywhere near the house made my heart ache for my parents. Now, seeing it as an adult, my stomach twisted for different reasons.

Hate and anger.

"C'mon." Uncle Randy grabbed my arm and pulled me out his side of the car once it was parked. I climbed out and yanked myself out of his grip, raising my chin in defiance. I wasn't a little girl anymore. He wouldn't overpower me with fear this time.

He stared down at me for a long moment, analyzing me, and laughed. "We'll see how long that bravery lasts." He gave me a shove toward the house, and I made my way up the porch steps and through the front door.

I walked down the hallway to the kitchen where two men sat at the table. The room hadn't been touched by the flames, but the smoke had damaged it enough for it to be redone. The soft-yellow paint my mother had loved so much had been changed to white. Simple and cold, much like my uncle.

Standing in the kitchen, all traces of my mother and father having been swept away with the greed of my uncle, I found myself standing taller, stronger. I wasn't the little girl he still thought I was. I wasn't going to let him get away with all that he'd done. This was my house. This was my land, and I was going to take it back, and he was going to pay for what he did.

"This her?" the man with a white scar running down his left cheek from eyelid to chin asked from the table. He wore a thick gold watch on his left wrist that matched the braided rope of necklace around his neck. He pointed a finger at me but kept his gaze on my uncle.

"My niece, Cherise." Randy nudged me.

I raised my chin and stared down scarface. His lips twisted up into a sneer, sending a dirty trickle down my spine.

"She's cute." He waggled his eyebrows.

"She'll sign everything over—"

"No, I won't." I cut him off. "I'm not signing anything."

Uncle Randy's face contorted. First surprise then raw anger built. His lip trembled, but I didn't have any false thinking that he was about to cry.

"You'll do what you're told, Cherise." He waved his sausage finger at me again. I never noticed how little like my father he actually looked. My father was fit and handsome, with thick black hair and masculine features. Uncle Randy had always been heavier than him, but now he bulged in every direction, and the fat of his face washed out the little resemblance there was. He'd lost half his hair since last I'd seen him. Regardless of the piss-poor comb-over, I could tell how little hair he actually had.

"This is my farm. This is my house, and I'm not signing anything over to you." I moved my gaze to settle directly in his line of sight. Scarface chuckled, but his partner, a similar-looking man with less stubble on his chin, did not.

"You own nothing. You'll do what you're told or—"

"Or what? You'll set me on fire, too?" I said, keeping my voice firm. It didn't matter how much my insides shook; I would not let him see my fear.

"I think you've said enough for the time being. You obviously need some time to think things through reasonably." Uncle Randy grabbed my arm, and, by his bulk alone, overpowered me, dragging me to the pantry in the far corner of the room.

My eyes set on the door, and panic ruled my actions. I pulled and smacked at him, but my fear had risen. He opened the pantry door and shoved me inside. I lunged for the opening, but the door slammed in my face, and I heard a bolt being thrown.

Why? Why would he have a lock on the pantry? When I was younger, he would wedge something on the other side to keep the door from opening. My parents didn't have a lock. But there was one now.

He'd known I would come back.

And he was prepared.

I pressed myself to the back shelves, knocking a can of vegetables to the floor with my elbow. Pulling the gun out of the bag, I held it in my hand, letting the weight of it push my fear away.

Dustan may not get to me in time. I had to deal with this on my own. I had to shove the childhood fears aside and stand on my feet now. I took slow breaths, focusing my attention on the feel of the gun in my hand. I had control. I had power. My uncle would not win this.

Uncle Randy may have been prepared for my abduction, but I was more prepared for my release.

I pulled slid back the rack on the gun, ready for him to open the door. I wouldn't hesitate this time.

DUSTAN

He had Cherise. I had known it the moment I opened the door to the room and she wasn't sitting on the edge of the bed waiting for me. A quick sweep of the room, I had realized she'd taken her bag—and the gun.

Getting past the gate at the farm wasn't a problem. I'd met up with my contact at the donut shop, and he'd given me all the pass codes I needed to maneuver around the farmhouse undetected. Only detection wasn't really an issue now.

I had known her uncle would hear of our arrival. Small towns had strong wagging tongues. But I hadn't thought he'd be so fucking bold coming for her in the bright light of the morning. My stomach rolled when I imagined him coming into the motel room, but I had to shove that shit away. I needed a clear head to get to her and get her out of there.

I punched the key into the gate and sped up the drive to the house. One man stood guard at the front door, wearing a hoody and a smug grin. He stepped forward when I climbed out of my car.

"Need something?" he asked, his beady gaze wandering over me, taking me in. I might not look like muscle with my pressed shirt and slacks, but he'd be surprised if he tried anything.

"Yeah. Cherise," I said, stomping up the steps straight for him. "She's inside, right?" I pointed at the screen door. He backed up as I got closer, his hand reaching into his pocket.

I rushed him, throwing my elbow into his throat then my knee connected with his stomach. He crumpled to the ground, gasping for air and holding his middle. I shoved him to his back with my foot, disgusted by how easily it was to throw him down.

Pressing my foot to his chest, I shoved off his hood.

"Fuck," I breathed. "You're a fucking kid!"

I'm sixteen, asshole." He coughed.

I shook my head and pointed my gun straight at him. Panic burst through his eyes; his mouth opened to start the endless begging.

"Shhh." I shook my head. "No noise."

"What do you want?" he asked, shoving at my foot and trying to wiggle free.

"Where's Cherise?"

"Kitchen." He closed his eyes, probably waiting for the bullet.

I pulled my foot back and kicked him hard enough to knock him out. "A fucking kid." I left him on the porch and flung the screen door open. I wasn't looking for a stealthy entrance.

The farmhouse was laid out in a simple manner; the kitchen could be seen from the front door. I watched the doorways, expecting to see more men. Overconfidence was a fatal mistake.

So was touching Cherise.

"Shane?"

"Sorry. He's taking a little nap." I walked into the kitchen, aiming my piece at the men at the table.

The one closest to me, with a white scar on his face, ran his tongue over his teeth while he studied me. The guy next to him started to move.

"No, no. Sit down, Carlos." The first man waved him down.

"You must be her little friend," Randy said from a corner of the room. He leaned against the counter with a cup of coffee in his hand.

"Yep, that's me. Where is she?" I asked, but from the corner of my eye I saw the door. A cold chill ran down me.

He followed my gaze.

"She's safe. Tucked away for now." The corner of his smug smile twitched.

"Randy, I don't have time for such drama," the man at the table spoke.

"No drama, Joseph. This asshole isn't a problem." Randy placed his cup on the counter and stepped toward me.

"He looks like a problem," Joseph said casually.

"You're fucking up a good thing here," Randy said. "I just need her signature. Then she can go. You both can."

Randy raised his hands as though to gesture that everything was fine, nothing was out of the ordinary.

I studied him for a minute, wondering if the

amount of stupidity I was seeing could actually be real. Or was he playing me, was this an act?

I glanced at the closed door.

"Cherise, you okay?" I called out.

"Yeah," a weak voice answered me. He had her fucking locked up again in that small room. I gripped the handle of my gun harder, but I kept my finger off the trigger.

"Bring her out here," I told him.

His gaze swung to Joseph, who gave a nod. "He wants her, get her."

Randy frowned. Maybe he thought his partners were going to let him keep her. So much stupidity, so much faith in bad people. It couldn't be real.

"He's opening the door, Cherise. Come out, okay?" I called, keeping my sights on Randy. "Just come out." If she'd managed to keep her Glock with her, I didn't want her shooting as he opened the door.

This was her kill, but I wanted that burden off her. I would take it. I would wear it for her to keep her safe from it.

"Go on, Randy, get her. We'll get her signatures then finish this mess." Joseph waved a hand.

Randy, seeming to finally get the idea he wasn't the alpha in this pack, shuffled to the door and slid the bolt. He yanked the door open.

A shot fired. Randy jerked back, falling against the counter, and stumbled back a step until slipping to the floor. Blood spurted from his neck, down his shirt. His fat hand pressed against the wound, his eyes wide with shock and pain.

I looked to the doorway. Cherise stepped out with her hand poised to take another shot. Her jaw set, her eyes focused on her uncle, she took cautious steps toward him until the toes of her shoes touched his leg.

"Darlin'," I said softly, trying to coax her attention.

She moved her aim slightly to the left and squeezed off another round, hitting him in the shoulder. His scream came out gurgled; the blood flowed faster through his fingers on his neck.

"Cherise," I said firmer.

She changed positions again, stepping between her uncle's legs, and standing directly over him.

"Look at me," she ordered him in a low, controlled tone.

His eyes rolled up.

"You thought me stupid and weak, and for a long time I believed that, too." She rolled her shoulders back, like prepping for the next move. "But not anymore." Her finger moved, and the last shot hit his face, obliterating any hope of recognition should there be need.

Blood splattered across the cabinets, the floor,

onto her, but she remained stoic. After the scent of gunpowder faded away, she dropped her hands to her sides and turned to face me.

"You good?" I asked, seeing the turmoil rolling into her features.

"Good." She nodded along with her lie.

"Well." Joseph stood from the table, along with Carlos. "That solves that problem."

Cherise turned her blood-splattered face toward the two men. "What problem is that?"

"Your uncle," Joseph answered. He took a step toward her. "He did believe you weak and stupid, but obviously he was very wrong about you." He pointed at the body on the kitchen floor.

"You're not one of his men," she said to him.

Joseph laughed. "No. I'm not."

"I won't deal with you." She rolled her shoulders back. I didn't reholster my gun, but I lowered my hands. She'd take the lead here, but I wasn't letting her go solo on it.

Joseph studied her for a long moment with narrowed eyes. "I have a good operation here."

"You mean my uncle's operation. You have a good crop coming from here," she countered. Strong girl. Good girl.

"True." Joseph nodded and swung his gaze to me. "His men are out back waiting for my word."

"You have control?" I asked.

He gave a small nod. "Randy has been stealing from me. Fucked with my scales and thought I wouldn't find out." He shook a finger at Cherise. "You solved a messy problem for me."

"You were going to kill him anyway?" she asked, and I heard the tinge of guilt, the little bite of her conscience starting to get into her mind.

"Eventually, but we needed this farm turned over

away from him," he said to her then turned back to me. "I never would have let him hurt her."

"You need her to hold the property."

"I need someone outside my family to hold the property. But it doesn't have to be her." He looked back at Carlos briefly. "Get the money."

"Money?" Cherise asked, her eyes wandering to her dead uncle.

"I'm buying the land from you," Joseph said plainly. "Christian, come in here," he called, and the back-porch door opened.

"Chris?" Cherise obviously recognized the lumberjack walking into the kitchen.

"Hey, Cherise," he said with a tight jaw then took in the sight of his boss huddled on the floor.

"Christian will be the owner."

Carlos came back into the kitchen with a bag and a folder, handing them both to Joseph. He placed the folder down on the table and presented her with a pen.

"Wait." I injected myself into the mix and pulled the papers from the table. Scanning them, I satisfied myself with the contents. Sales papers. The house and land were owned outright. She needed only to make a cash sale and turn over the property.

"I'll be done with this?" Cherise asked me. The droplets of blood dried on her cheek.

"You'll be done. The entire property will belong to him."

"But if Joseph is paying—"

"That's not our business, darlin'. Just take care of this one thing then we're gone. It's over." I kept her gaze focused on me and plucked the pen from Joseph and handed it to her.

"And Uncle…"

"Taken care of," Joseph assured her.

Her fingers brushed mine as she took the pen. I

stepped to the side and shielded her from the other men in the room as she read over the document and scribbled her name in all the right places. I doubted she understood what she read with the adrenaline starting to wear off and the exhaustion from the events creeping in, but I didn't comment.

She didn't ask about the amount of money in the bag, and I didn't offer the question, either. The official sale price was much less than whatever was in that bag, but no comments were made about it.

Carlos handed the bag to me, and I pulled Cherise to my side. She'd switched her gun to her left hand but still clung to it like a safety blanket. I wouldn't take it away from her just yet.

"There. Done." Joseph smiled. I'd met plenty of scheming, slimy assholes in my work, but Joseph didn't give off that vibe. I'm not saying he was a good guy, fuck no, far from it, but he would honor the sale and he'd leave Cherise alone.

"I need to also thank you, Dustan." He raised his eyes to meet mine. "Antonio was my uncle. Another problem needed to be resolved. You have my gratitude."

I nodded. Not engaging in conversation would get us in my car and out of there much sooner.

"We can go?" Cherise asked. I could sense her pulling away and retreating into herself. I needed to get her away and alone before it happened. If she was going to roll away into a panic attack, we needed to be away from here.

"By all means." Joseph gestured.

I eyeballed the room one more time and peeked down the hallway, assuring myself we'd have no trouble. But Joseph was a man of his word, and we walked out of the house and drove away without incident.

CHERISE

"I killed him," I whispered.

Dustan nodded. "Yeah, darlin', you did." He dipped a washcloth into the bathtub and brought it back up to my face.

I was naked and sitting in a warm bath full of bubbles. I'd killed my uncle, and Dustan was giving me a bath.

"He deserved killing," I said, not stopping him from wiping the coarse cloth across my cheek.

"That he did," he agreed.

I grabbed his wrist when he started to clean my other cheek and pulled his gaze to mine. "I don't regret it. I'm not sorry."

He studied me for a long minute. Those dark eyes of his burrowed into mine before his lips gentled and curved. "Nothing to be sorry for."

I nodded and closed my eyes. The longer I waited for the sinister wave of remorse to roll in, the less I felt about the situation. Maybe I was in shock.

"You didn't want me to shoot him. I heard it in your voice when I was in the pantry." I opened my eyes.

"I didn't want you to carry the weight of it," he said and dropped the cloth into the water. The bubbles had eased into small patches floating on the top surface of the water, which had taken a pink tint.

"I was bad, then?" I asked.

He laughed. "No, darlin', you were good. Real good. Perfect." He cupped my chin and dragged my face up to meet his lips. Warm and soothing.

"I'm really sleepy," I said a moment before a yawn escaped me.

"You'll have to sleep in the car. We need to get on the road," he said gently. I didn't like the soft hands treatment.

"I'm okay, Dustan." I tried to reassure him, but all I got back was a smile. "I'm telling you the truth. I'm fine."

He reached behind me and unplugged the tub. "I know."

"Does that piss you off? That I'm not falling apart?" I asked, feeling annoyance starting to overtake the exhaustion.

He moved to his feet and settled a glare on me. "I'm not pissed off. I'm wanting to get on the road." He reached down and hoisted me to my feet, holding onto my arms as I stepped out of the tub.

I snatched the towel from his hand. "I'll get dressed, then. I need my bag."

He walked out of the bathroom and tossed the

bag on the counter. Without another glance, he pulled the door shut and left me alone. I hugged the towel to my body and closed my eyes. His wall was back up, isolating himself from me.

I dried off and dressed quickly, wanting to put this place as far behind me as possible. I dug through the bag and noticed he'd removed the Glock.

When I flung open the bathroom door, Dustan stood at the door with his arms crossed over his chest. "Ready?"

"Can I get my shoes on first?" I snapped.

"Temper, temper, darlin'," he said softly, but the words were empty.

"Fuck that." I snagged my shoes and stomped to the little table and chairs at the back of the room. Plopping down in the chair, I dropped the shoes to the floor. "You know, maybe it's better if you just go."

"Go?" His tone lowered with his question.

"Yeah." I looked up from wiggling my foot into the shoe. "Just go. I can get a cab to the airport and fly back to Chicago." Each word stabbed at my insides.

"You think we're done?" He closed in, reminding me of how hulking his presence could be.

"I think you're mad because of what I did, and I don't need that right now. Right now, I need to get home, to my own fucking bed, try to get my job back if possible, and forget today even happened." All of those things on my list were nothing more than a daydream, but I was grabbing at straws. Not sure where I stood, or how I got where I was because I didn't want him to drop me at an airport. I didn't want him to walk out of that motel room without me.

"You think I'm mad because you pulled the trigger?" He kicked the second shoe away from me and hauled me to my feet. His fingers dug into my shoulders, and he gave me a small shake.

"You're pissed about something."

"I am," he agreed. "I'm pissed because I let my guard down for a minute and your uncle got you. I'm pissed because I didn't stop him from taking you in the first fucking place. I'm pissed because you didn't need me to save you at all. But, most of all, I'm pissed because it all could have gone sideways in a snap of a finger, and I could have lost you."

He yanked me to him, his lips crushing down over mine. I pushed against him at first, but he wouldn't relent. Slowly, I eased into his hold, melted beneath the warmth of his kiss.

He would always be a force to deal with; he'd pull me along and, no matter how much I pushed him away—he'd charge back in. I could sense it now. When he marked me the night before, when he claimed me as his, he wasn't talking about the moment. He meant permanency.

I gasped when he broke the kiss and his dark eyes stared down me. My lip trembled, the emotions of the day finally crashing into me with the furiousness of a hurricane.

"You didn't lose me."

"No." He pressed a kiss to my lips. "I didn't."

"But if I stay with you—"

"It's not easy, being with me," he said, pressing his forehead against mine.

"Maybe I could help," I whispered. He was unguarded for the moment, and I didn't want to give him reason to throw that wall back up.

He chuckled. "If I never see you holding a gun again, it will be too fucking soon, darlin'."

"You can't lock me away."

"No." He pulled back, sucking in a long breath. "You're not meant for a cage." He brushed his fingers along my temple, pushing my hair from my face.

"Then what happens here, Dustan?" I sank back into my seat.

"We take the next step, and then the next, we just keep moving until we find the pace that works for us."

"That doesn't sound like much of an answer." I frowned.

He shook his head and tapped two fingers beneath my chin. "It's the best one we have right now. The only thing that's sure is you aren't leaving me, and I'm not leaving you."

"And if I change my mind?" I bit down on my bottom lip, feeling sarcasm tingling on my tongue. He was ramped up from the energy of the day. Testing his patience probably wouldn't go well for me.

"I'll change it back." He flicked my chin with his fingers and stepped back. "Get that shoe on so we can get on the road. I'm not stopping till we're home and I can get you naked in my bed."

I pointed to the bed beside him. "There's one right here."

"Yes. And there's a drug cartel boss five miles away. I'd prefer more than that between us." He walked away from me, but the telltale sign of his hard cock jutting against the zipper of his slacks gave me some satisfaction.

Things weren't going to be normal with us. We probably wouldn't be having dinner at TGI Fridays anytime in the near future and catching a double feature at the movies.

I'd walked into that bar weeks ago trying to get myself out of my shell. Turned out Dustan had better ways. He showed me the strength I didn't know I had, taught me the power I held inside, and gave me the freedom to unleash it.

I didn't need a self-help book.

I just needed Dustan.

EPILOGUE
DUSTAN

"There he is." I watched the black Corvette ease into the covered garage and head toward us.

"I know, I know...stay in the car." Cherise rolled her eyes at me and pulled the visor down to look in the mirror.

"I mean it, darlin'. Don't be bad tonight."

She snapped the visor back up in place and gifted me with one of her sarcastic grins. "I wouldn't dream of it. It's the first night you actually took me out of that apartment."

We'd been back in Chicago for a week, but I didn't want her gallivanting around the city yet. Not until the last loose end was taken care of.

I eyed her. "I love that fucking dress." She'd grumbled when I handed it to her that afternoon, but I'd been right. Her curves were killing me in it. "Maybe going out was a bad idea," I mumbled.

"You promised," she reminded me in her sweet singsong voice. She was trying to be good, but if I pushed her anymore, she'd unleash the snark. And the snark would get her more riled up, and I'd have a full-blown bad girl on my hands.

"Stay here." I pointed my finger at her and popped open my door. I heard her huff and smiled to myself.

My boots sounded as I made my way over to Bobby's car. He rolled down his window as I arrived at the car, and I could make out his pistol lying in his lap.

"Hey." I gave a curt nod. "You have the information I asked for?"

"Sure do." He stuck an envelope through the window. "Thought you might like to know the Merde family has called off all searches for your girl there." He gestured toward my car. I hadn't heard the door open.

Cherise stood in front of my door, one ankle crossed over the other and her arms crossed over her chest. Her hair blew around her face. The empty lot made a wind tunnel with the cool evening breeze.

She took my noticing her as leave to join us, and her heels clicked along the concrete.

"Hi." She smiled down at Bobby and tucked a strand of hair behind her ear. "You must be Bobby."

"You must be Cherise," he said, looking from her to me.

"Well, we're just heading to dinner. Thanks for this." I tapped the top of his car with the folder he'd handed me. Bullshit intel on a random target that I didn't need.

"Shit, my phone." Cherise giggled and turned

away from us, digging through her purse.

"Oh, here it is." She stepped back to the car and produced a pineapple hand grenade. With little effort, she pulled the pin and dropped it onto the floorboard of Bobby's car.

My heart skyrocketed into my throat. Throbbing silence filled a beat, and then I grabbed her arm. We ran, my legs pumping hard to get us away from the car before the grenade went off.

"Fuck!" Bobby's scream echoed just before the blast. The force of the explosion threw us to the ground, but I scrambled back up and pulled my naughty girl with me.

She looked over her shoulder at the fire, the black smoke billowing from the car, and her eyes widened, a small scrape on her cheek from hitting the ground with the force of the blow, a reminder of her wickedness.

"I told you to stay put," I chastised as we rushed.

"I know." She nodded toward the car. Even at the late hour, there would be no hiding the damage. I'd already worked on the security cameras in the lot; we just needed to get the hell out of there.

She jogged around the back and got inside, still staring at the blaze she'd caused.

I turned the ignition and peeled away, heading for the exit ramps.

"You left it in the car," she tried to explain as I drove through the back alleys, getting us farther away faster.

"I had another in my pocket. That was the spare." I changed gears effortlessly.

"Oh."

"Uh-huh. *Oh* is right." I flashed her a grin. Her hair blew wildly around her with the window cracked but the brightness in her eyes, the life bubbling in her grin, took most of the irritation away. Most. Not all.

"You were a bad girl, darlin'." I turned us onto the stretch of highway that would take us to the apartment. She'd lost the privilege of a night out on the town.

"I know," she said with a smile, her lower lip tucked between her teeth.

"And what happens to bad girls?" I asked, touching her bare knee. Fuck, that dress was too much. I'd have to keep it locked up for special occasions.

She leaned over the middle console and bit down on my earlobe. "Really bad things."

"That's right, darlin'."

CAVALIERI DELLA MORTE

Beautifully Brutal - Dani René
http://bit.ly/BeautifullyBrutalTBR

Vow of Obedience - Brianna Hale
http://bit.ly/VowOfObedienceTBR

Martyris - Yolanda Olson
http://bit.ly/MartyrisTBR

His Salvation - Claire Marta
http://bit.ly/HisSalvationTBR

Ivy's Poison - India R Adams
http://bit.ly/IvysPoisonTBR

A Cruel Love - S.M. Soto
http://bit.ly/ACruelLoveTBR

Darkest Deeds - Cora Kenborn
http://bit.ly/DarkestDeeds_TBR

CAVALIERI DELLA MORTE

Scarlet Mark - Lexi C. Foss
http://bit.ly/ScarletMarkTBR

Delinquent - Ally Vance
http://bit.ly/DelinquentTBR

Redemption - Anna Edwards
http://bit.ly/RedemptionTBR

Valor - Measha Stone
http://bit.ly/ValorTBR

Sorrow's Queen - Ashleigh Giannoccaro
http://bit.ly/SorrowsQueenTBR

Inexorable - Jo-Anne Joseph
http://bit.ly/InexorableTBR

A SNEAK PEEK AT SORROW'S QUEEN BY ASHLEIGH GIANNOCCARO & MURPHY WALLACE

SORROW

I hate New York, every part of it, the entire state can fuck right off the damn map. I cannot believe the little bitch has been hiding in Queens if her and her mother thought they'd be able to hide forever they're fools. I'm like a bloodhound when it comes to sniffing out the fox I'm hunting. She's running about town like there's no one nipping at her heels, going to school and having her nails done. Naive. She's being hunted, and I am sick of the chase. I hate being here, the minute I have her we are leaving this hell hole.

For the life of me, I can't wrap my head around this job, what this girl has that Marcus King could possibly want. Other than probably her baby teeth and virginity I just don't get it. He's in his fifties, she turns eighteen in six weeks. There are other, much easier ways of catching a young wife — it's not like he doesn't have women throwing themselves at his feet already. Why make me chase the one that wants nothing to do with him halfway across the country? Ever heard of mail-order brides? You can get a real hottie from Russia that can't talk back because she doesn't know English. That would be easier than this.

My burner phone buzzes in the center console of the car, it can only be Arthur or one of my brothers.

Check on Gareth.

I'm in Queens trying to catch King's future wife. Ask Lance to stop by. I type a quick reply.

The school bell just rang, signaling the end of the school day and I am not missing my chance to grab the little Queenie from Queens and get the fuck out of town.

The phone vibrates in my hand before I can put it down.

There's a wedding in six weeks — she better be there. Do not let me down, Tristan.

There it is, the unspoken truth. Arthur is just waiting for me to fail him. One mistake and you're on his list, his eyes on your every move. No room to mess up, I won't do it again. Letting him down isn't an option, I am going to prove myself to him.

I watch Queen Sophie as she exits the school gates, she turns left and heads right towards where I am parked just far enough away that no one will notice me. I have been watching her for two weeks, I know she will walk alone. Reading a book. She has no friends here — she's not like these kids. Her plaid skirt is two inches too short, and the matching headband that keeps her raven locks off her pretty face makes her look like jailbait. She is jail bait. That Catholic school girl look might be what Marcus is after — bet your life if she wasn't a kid or my mark, I'd push her up against a wall and have my way with her. Standing against my car now, the afternoon sun broiling me, I wait until she is two steps away, then I open the back door of my rented BMW. I made sure the child lock is on, so once she's in she can't get out again.

"Sophie," I say stepping right in front of her, she crashes into me. I grab her wrist and before she can scream or kick up a fuss she's in the car, and I'm slamming the door closed. People are so slow to realize when they're in danger — when the predator is right beside them they still can't smell it.

Her book falls into the dirty gutter water running beside my car, I don't bother trying to save it. I need to move quickly before anyone sees us, or hears her. I get into the driver's side of the car, and start it, quickly merging into the after school traffic. Sophie is screaming and banging on the glass partition between us. I chose a chauffeur car, for this exact reason. I don't want to get all scratched up, those talons on her fingers would do some damage. She's kicking the glass now like a maniac. It's a long drive all the way across the country. We don't fly with people we've kidnapped — it's risky. We're in for a twenty-one-hour drive without stopping, so the next two days will give her enough time cool off, or pass out. I turn up the music to drown out her wailing and get on the freeway. As soon as I know we're not being followed, I pick up the burner phone and call Arthur.

"Tristan." He greets me, in his usual flat tone. Not a hint of emotion in his voice. There's no way to tell if he's murderous or happy.

"I have the girl. She's a bit feral, but it's long drive she'll have time to calm down." I look in the mirror at her. "Should I expect trouble from the cops?"

"No, her family won't report her missing. You should have clean sailing all the way here."

"See you in two or three days."

"I'll be waiting." He answers before cutting the call. She is no longer screaming like a banshee, instead, she is trying to murder me with her eyes. Her death glare is so cute it's almost funny. I laugh at her in the mirror. The penny has obviously dropped, I watch her digging in her backpack for her phone. She can call anyone she wants, no one is coming to save her. This arrangement was made between her father and Marcus. She doesn't get a choice, her parents will not step in and stop it, that would be suicide.

"Daddy." I hear her cry into the phone. I turn the music down, listening to her side of the exchange.

"What's going on? You told me that you'd fix this." She sobs.

"He's a sick old pervert." Her voice rises an octave.

"I'll kill myself. I'm telling you now. I will slit my wrists before I marry that wrinkly old bastard." She listens for a few moments, her breaths heavy and ragged.

"I hate you! I fucking hate you!" She screams before hurling her phone against the glass that separates us. She cries now, the tantrum replaced with emotional sobs. They get under my thick skin, as I listen to her breaking. The problem with being born into the underworld is you have no choice, your family is a part of this. Her birthright was always to be promised to a powerful man to strengthen family ties. Her father just picked a really shitty one for her. The way her eyes beg me to save her plays into the small soft part of me that isn't completely lost to what I do for a living. For a second I consider letting her get away, but that would be like signing my own death certificate. Not delivering is not an option.

Eventually, she lies down on the backseat, I can still hear her sniffling, but I can't see her face. I take the chance, turn the music up again, and work on putting up the tall barriers around my emotions. There's no room for feelings in this job, because if you have empathy for one person, how can you turn around and kill the next one. The afternoon turns into the haziness of dusk and soon the sun is gone completely. The streetlights and black sky calling me home, downing two energy drinks and shifting around in my seat. I settle myself to drive until we get to a designated motel for a quick rest.

My eyelids have been heavy for the last hundred miles, and the shitty pink motel sign is the most welcome sight in the early hours of the morning. We'll stop here for a few hours of sleep, a shower and a hot breakfast. I park the car and flash my lights three times. After a few minutes, the desk clerk Larry comes out and hands me the key to room nine through the window.

"Sorrow. Haven't seen you in these parts for years. I was surprised when they said it was you coming." He says, smiling at me with his one missing front tooth and saggy eyelids.

"Good to see you, Larry," I say taking the key. "You busy tonight? This one might make noise."

"Only one room full and it's upstairs at the other end of the corridor. You should be good. If anyone complains I'll deal with it."

"Thanks, man," I say.

"See you for breakfast then?" He asks me, shoving his hands in the pockets of his grubby jeans.

"Sure thing." He nods and disappears back into his office. I move the car so it's parked right in front of room nine, out of sight of the road and passers-by. I know she's awake, but she's still laying down. I open the glass that separates us, just enough that I can talk to her.

"We're stopping for the night. I'd really like if this wasn't a fucking ordeal, so let's go inside like civilized adults, please. No one will hear you scream and if you run I will shoot you. The caretaker is paid very well to turn a blind eye, so you're not getting saved here. Think you can be a big girl and walk the three feet to the door?" She's sitting up now, looking at me with tired, swollen eyes.

"If I say no?"

"Then I grab you, put you over my shoulder and drag you inside anyway." She swallows, then licks her dry lips. "There's no option where you win, there's just an easy way and a hard way to do what I want."

"I'm not going to do anything you want, so I

guess there'll be a lot of hard-way going on."

Jesus, really? I would rather be doing anything than this job I swear.

"Fine." I sigh.

ABOUT THE AUTHOR

USA Today Bestselling Author Measha Stone is a lover of all things erotic and fun who writes kinky romantic suspense and dark romance novels. She won the 2018 Golden Flogger award in two categories, Best Advanced BDSM and Best Anthology. She's hit #1 on Amazon in multiple categories in the U.S. and the U.K. When she's not typing away on her computer, she can be found nestled up with a cup of tea and her kindle.

ALSO BY THE AUTHOR

EVER AFTER
Beast
Tower
Red

GIRLS OF THE ANNEX
Daddy Ever After

BLAIRE'S WORLD
Kristoff

OWNED AND PROTECTED
Protecting His Pet
Protecting His Runaway
His Captive Pet
His Captive Kitten

Becoming His Pet

BLACK LIGHT SERIES
Black Light Valentine Roulette
Black Light Cuffed
Black Light Roulette Redux
Black Light Suspicion
Black Light Celebrity Roulette

UNTIL SERIES
Until You a novella
Until Daddy

WINDY CITY
Hidden Heart
Secured Heart
Indebted Heart
Liberated Heart

Printed in Great Britain
by Amazon